Puffin Books
The Bonny Pit Laddie

All his life Dick Ullathorne had expected to follow his father and brother into the mine. Mining seemed the only natural employment for boys in the pit village where he lived, where people could hear dull subterranean sounds below the floors of their houses, and boys explored ancient, deserted shafts as one of their entertainments.

Dick had never questioned this way of life until the night Mr Sleath, the owner of the mine, was taken ill and Dick had to help him home. That set him wondering by what right Mr Sleath lived so well and held such power over his workers' lives.

Other people were wondering that too, but it took the heartbreaking starvation of a bitter strike and a dangerous pit accident to make Dick break loose from the pit for his future.

The Bonny Pit Laddie, published in hardback in 1960, was one of the first children's books to portray working people in a sympathetic and totally realistic way. It has lost none of its freshness and was a recent winner of The Other Award. Frederick Grice was singled out by the judges to the award for his 'historical accuracy, credible characters and an ability to bring vividly to life his stories of ordinary people and their difficulties. His books are particularly memorable for the tenacity and courage of their young heroes who must struggle hard to achieve the future they want.'

This is the first appearance of *The Bonny Pit Laddie* in paperback.

Also published in Puffins: *The Courage of Andy Robson*.

FREDERICK GRICE

The Bonny Pit Laddie

ILLUSTRATED BY
BRIAN WILDSMITH

PUFFIN BOOKS
IN ASSOCIATION WITH
OXFORD UNIVERSITY PRESS

Puffin Books, Penguin Books Ltd, Harmondsworth, Middlesex, England
Viking Penguin Inc., 40 West 23rd Street, New York, New York 10010, U.S.A.
Penguin Books Australia Ltd, Ringwood, Victoria, Australia
Penguin Books Canada Ltd, 2801 John Street, Markham, Ontario, Canada L3R 1B4
Penguin Books (N.Z.) Ltd, 182–190 Wairau Road, Auckland 10, New Zealand

First published by Oxford University Press 1960
Published in Puffin Books 1980
Reprinted 1982, 1983, 1986

Typeset, printed and bound in Great Britain by
Hazell Watson & Viney Limited,
Member of the BPCC Group,
Aylesbury, Bucks
Set in Monotype Ehrhardt

To
all the people of the colliery
in which I was born

Contents

The bonny pit laddie, the canny pit laddie,
The bonny pit laddie for me, O.
He sits on his cracket, and hews in his jacket,
And brings the white siller to me, O.

Old Durham song

I

Dick and Kit

Richard Ullathorne's father was a miner and lived in Branton Colliery. When you gave your address you had to remember the word 'colliery' because there were two Brantons. One was the village that stood on the ridge of the hill above the Rushy Field, and was made up of two rows of old houses so far apart that the space between them was not so much a street as a long village green. Some of the houses were falling down because the colliery workings now ran under the village. Once when Dick was sitting in one of them with his mother he heard a dull sound under the floor, and Mrs Lee who lived there said it was the sound of shots being fired in the seams under the village.

The colliery where Dick lived was spread out on the slopes below the village, and was separated from it by fields and stretches of common land. One of these was the Rushy Field where the band used to play on fine Sunday nights in the summer. There was one old row of stone houses not far away from the railway that Dick always liked; but his mother always thanked God they didn't live there. His father said that these old stone houses had been put up for the sinkers when they were making the shaft. All the other rows in the colliery were of brick, and Dick knew the names of every one of them, starting from

9

Cobden Terrace at the bottom and going to Church Street at the top. They were all laid out in hard, straight lines, and the spaces between them were just coaly earth, dusty in summer and miry in winter. To the south of these streets stood the pithead with its yards, sidings and workshops, and from it a little railway line led up an incline to the depots where the miners' housecoal was tipped into carts to be delivered up and down the streets. In wet weather the horses sank up to their fetlocks in the mud.

On the north side of the colliery stood the school, a gaunt clay-coloured brick building with tall narrow windows like a church. With its ugly shape and muddy colour and dull green doors it looked more like a prison than a school.

It was entirely surrounded by a high wall that was easy to climb on to but difficult to walk along, because the top was rounded. The playground was a bumpy clayey area, channelled by the rain until it looked like one of those contour maps Dick's class had once tried to make with Mr Roderick. In the corners, the parts not played on, wild barley grew in clumps, and the boys used to push the ears up the sleeves of their jackets and work their arms about until the spiky heads came out under their armpits. The thin grass blades you could put between your thumbs and blow. If you blew the right way you could make a noise like a parrot screeching. On one side of the yard lay the colliery allotments with fences made of flattened bath-tins, old sleepers and even old bedsteads. Mr Ullathorne had one of these allotments, but the only thing about it that Dick liked was the border of London Pride. On the other side of the school ran the single-line railway that connected the main pithead with the drifts higher up on the fells.

When Dick was busy with his lessons he often heard the little engine that they called the 'tankie' puffing up the heavy slopes or racketing downhill around the sharp curves. Dick had once heard his father say that if Jonty (that was the name of the engine-driver) didn't watch he'd jump the tankie off the rails one of these fine days; and for a long time after that Dick had held his breath when he heard the engine whistling past the school.

Every school-day began in the same way, with the repetition of arithmetic tables. While the repetition was going on the Headmaster had all the partitions in the large room thrown back so that he could keep an eye on every pupil. He was a large man, with a roll of fat on his shoulders which gave him the appearance of being hunched, and his heavy chin sagged over his collar. He stood behind his dais like a general and Dick always had the feeling that he was taking part in a military review or a parade such as they had on Empire Day. When Mr Allcroft gave the signal he joined with the rest in the familiar sing-song –

Once two is two
Two twos are four
Three twos are six
Four twos are eight . . .

The Headmaster looked from right to left as they chanted, trying to spot the shirkers. Dick went through the tables mechanically, looking round at the familiar furniture of the classroom, the framed certificate from the Missionary Society, the picture of the Products of Ceylon, and the dark wall map of the British Isles, with the names of all the capes and bays sprouting out of it. As one of the cleverer boys he had a seat in one of the back desks near the pipes, but when he edged back a little to touch them with his calves he found they were cold. At last they got to the twelve-times table, and the chanting grew a little louder. After the last line –

Twelve twelves are a hundred and forty-four –

Mr Allcroft gave another signal, the creaking and varnished partitions were pulled across, and the class teachers took over.

There was a spell of 'mental', and then they were set to work on problems. They all worked on slates, and every now and then a slate pencil would screech across a slate and set Dick's teeth on edge. However, he was a fast worker, and he soon finished his problems. He was just going to tell Mr Roderick that he had finished when a door in the partition opened and a boy came in with a note. Mr Roderick read it, looked up and called out, 'Richard Ullathorne! Ullathorne! Where is he? Ah, yes. Mr Allcroft wants to see you. Come on, lad. Don't look thunderstruck. Get a move on.'

Dick started up from his seat in great fear. If the Chief Constable or the Public Executioner had sent for him he could not have been more alarmed. There passed quickly through his mind all the misdeeds of which he could remember being guilty in the last few weeks – climbing on the school wall, copying from Jo Basey, shouting down the steps at the boiler-man, flashing a mirror in the music lesson. If the Headmaster wanted to see him, it was, of course, to cane him. He expected to be caned, and began to wonder how many he would get. He put his hand in his pocket, took out from a tin the horsehair that he had pulled out of his grandmother's settee, and wrapped it furtively

12

round the middle finger of his right hand. Jo Basey said it would make the cane split.

The Headmaster looked at him over his glasses, and blew twice down his nostrils. He always gave two little snorts like this, as if he was preparing to charge.

'Are you Richard Ullathorne?'

'Yes, sir.'

'Why isn't your brother Christopher at school?'

'I don't know, sir.'

'What do you mean by saying you don't know? He is your brother, isn't he?'

'Yes, sir.'

'You both live at the same address, don't you?'

'Yes, sir.'

'Well, don't be obstinate, boy. What's the matter with him?'

'Please, sir, I don't know, sir. I haven't seen him since last Wednesday.'

'You haven't seen him? You must have a big house if one member of the family never sees the other. Where do you live?'

'Twenty-three Chapel Row, sir.'

'That's not exactly a mansion, is it?'

Richard did not reply.

'What are you holding your tongue for, boy?'

'Please, sir, I'm not sure what a mansion is.'

'Well, you should be. You've read the Bible, haven't you? "In my Father's house are many mansions." Have you never heard that verse? A mansion is a large house. What are you frowning at?'

'I can't understand it, sir. I can't understand how a house can have large houses in it.'

'What? Now, don't be argumentative, Ullathorne. Where's this brother of yours? You know he's playing truant, don't you?'

'Please, sir, he's gone off somewhere.'

'Yes, but where?'

'Please, sir, we don't know.'

'How do you mean – "We don't know"?'

'My father doesn't know.'

'Doesn't anybody know?'

'No, sir, but we think he's gone off with the scoury-stone man again.'

'With the what?'

'The scoury-stone man, the man that comes round with scoury-stone for jam-jars.'

'And does your father let him do things like this?'

'No, sir, but he can't stop him. He gets mad with him, though.'

'He gets mad, does he? Well, just you tell your father that if he gets m— – I suppose you mean "angry" – then I'm going to get even angrier. Just you tell your father that if that brother of yours can stay away from his own home as long as he likes, he cannot stay away from my school. And you can tell him that when your Christopher comes home, two things are going to happen. The first is that Twenty-three Chapel Row will have a visit from the School Board Man. And the second is that your brother will get from me the biggest hiding that any boy in this school has ever got.'

'Yes, sir.'

'And don't you go away, yet. I have a few more questions to ask you now that you're here.'

Dick gripped his right hand and made sure that the

14

horsehair was still around his finger. He felt that Mr Allcroft was going to ask him the definition of an adverb, and
that was one thing he could never get right. To his great
relief, however, the Headmaster chose arithmetic.

'What's a hundred pence?'

'Six and . . . Eight and fourpence, sir.'

'How many yards in one rod, pole, or perch?'

'Five and a half, sir.'

He felt flushed with success, and almost eager for more
questions, but the Headmaster looked a little disappointed
at not being given an excuse to be angry.

'Hmm . . . at any rate you've saved yourself the stick.
But your brother will catch it and you can tell him so.
Now run along.'

'Yes, sir. Thank you, sir.'

And he hurried off keeping a good hold on his horsehair
thread. You never knew when you were going to need a
thing like that.

For the rest of the day Dick was very careful to keep
out of trouble, and whenever he found himself near Mr
Allcroft he looked away and hoped that he would not be
noticed. He kept hoping that Kit would come home, so
that he could face the music himself; but once Kit disappeared there was no knowing where he had gone and
how long he would be away. Kit had been sent to every
school in the district but there was no Headmaster that
could stop him from playing truant. Mr Ullathorne had
even sent him once to the Catholic School, hoping that the
Head there, who was the strictest schoolmaster for miles
around, would be able to tame him, but in the end he had
been compelled to ask Mr Allcroft to take him back.

As soon as Dick had had his tea he went out. There was

always something to do in the colliery streets; there was always some gang or other up to mischief. He jumped over the yard gate, and there at the top of the street he saw Bobby Keegan and Frankie Clennel examining something under the street-lamp. When he got up to them he saw that it was an old bucket pierced like a brazier, and he knew that they were going to the Fiery Heap to get fire.

The Fiery Heap was their name for the big slag heap that curled around the colliery and seemed to guard it from the rest of the world. Many years ago it had caught fire, and though from time to time attempts had been made to put it out, nothing could extinguish it completely. By day it fumed and smouldered, and wisps of blue and yellow flame travelled up its steep edges until they wavered and mingled in the smoky air. By night it glowed, and

when a keen wind played upon it, it burst into flames, into purple and orange tongues that licked hungrily upward. The boys liked to fill buckets with the red-hot core, and take them back into the streets.

'Stand out of the way!' cried Frankie when he had filled his bucket. 'I'm ganna swing it!'

He sent it backwards and forwards a few times, then whirled it over his head and round in a full circle. As it swung through the cold air the cinders roared into new life, and the whole brazier began to blaze. The boys then passed a stick through the handle and carried the fire like a sacrifice back to the street.

Neither Chapel Row nor Russell Street which stood opposite it had proper lavatories. Instead ash-closets in groups of five were ranged in the space between the two rows. It was against one of these blocks that the boys stopped, raising the fire from the ground with the help of broken bricks, and squatting on their haunches or 'unkers', as they called them, in a circle around it.

It was a murky night and the sky was overcast. The blackened walls of the houses and yards and privies seemed to sweat, and the street had been churned into a muddy paste. But the boys noticed none of this. They crouched round their fire like tribesmen, watching the flames lick through the holes, feeding them with coal from the nearest coal-houses, and telling strange stories of gamekeepers who lived in the valley and fired at them from behind the bushes, of monkey-men who chased them over the Heap, of tramps and schoolmasters and policemen. They stole potatoes and roasted them, and enjoyed the warmth and the secrecy and the redness until their mothers were heard calling shrilly for them to come in –

'Dick . . . y!'

'Frank . . . ie! Come in here this minute!'

They lingered as long as they could, but at last they had to go. They kicked the bucket over and watched the ashes sizzle in the wet mud, and reluctantly went in.

As soon as Dick came into the kitchen he knew that something had happened. His mother was short-tempered and his father's brows were down; and his brother's boots, caked with mud, were drying on the hearth.

2

The City

'Off to bed! Off to bed!' said Dick's father to him. 'If you cannot come home in decent time for a meal you can go hungry. Upstairs there, and not another word out of you.'

Normally Dick would have stayed and tried to argue, but he knew that Kit would be waiting for him. He kicked off his boots and got upstairs as fast as he could; and, as he expected, his brother was sitting on the bed examining, by the light of a candle, the contents of his pockets. It was not the first time Kit had 'played the nick' from both home and school. During the last few years he had become an incorrigible wanderer. Nothing could keep him at home for long; when the urge came upon him he would vanish and no one knew where he had got to. Neither his father nor his mother could do anything with him, and no punishment could deter him from decamping. He seemed a born vagabond.

'Did you get wrong this time?' asked Dick.

'No.'

'What did my da say?'

'He told me off.'

'But where have you been?'

'I've been with Enoch.'

'The scoury-stone man?'

'That's him. Here, get into bed, kidder, and I'll tell you.'

They both climbed into bed and pulled the bed-clothes up to their chins. This was the moment that Dick liked best, when in the warm and cosy bed in the little attic he could lie and listen to Kit's stories.

'Where did he take you, Kit?'

'We went up to Towin Law. That's where Enoch gets his scoury-stone. And there was a coursin' meetin' there, on the fells.'

'What's a coursing meeting?'

'Greyhounds chasing hares. Enoch said they were sure to want beaters, so we stopped there.'

'Were you a beater?'

'You bet I was. You have to get yourself a stick and wallop the heather, and when the hares run out the men slip the dogs. Lad, it's grand sport. Them greyhounds, Dick, they can travel. They gan like the wind.'

'But where did you sleep?'

'Enoch knows plenty places. Do you know, Dick, right

up on the fells there's a signal cabin. It isn't used now. We stopped in there.'

'Where did you get washed?'

'Washed? Here, talk with some sense, lad. Enoch never gets washed. But we got paid for beating. I got ninepence a day from the men with the dogs. I've still got it, and do you know what I'm ganna do with it? I'm ganna buy a dog. I'm ganna buy a greyhound.'

'My mother will never let you keep a greyhound here.'

'I'll keep it at Enoch's, and we'll set it after hares. Would you like a greyhound, kidder?'

'I would.'

'Just watch, kidder. I'll buy a greyhound, and then I'll buy a horse and trap, and we'll both sell scoury-stone, eh, Dick?'

So they talked on, until the door at the foot of the stairs was suddenly wrenched open, and their father shouted up to them:

'For heaven's sake stop talking up there! If ye dinna get yourselves off to sleep I'll take my belt to the pair of you!'

They knew that it was no more than a threat, for no matter how badly his boys behaved David Ullathorne never struck them; but they respected his anger. They lowered their voices and fell asleep, and in his dreams Dick drove his beautiful black and yellow trap through the waving heather, and at his side loped a greyhound, white and obedient.

Kit, like his mother, was a good waker. The following morning he was up first, and she could hear him chopping the sticks for the fire and whistling. He always whistled. His mother often poked fun at him and called him 'Whistling Rufus', but he never minded being chaffed. He whistled as a bird whistles, from the pleasure of being alive, and although she teased him, his mother loved him for it. It was difficult not to love Kit and not to forgive him. By the end of the morning when he had shovelled in the coals for her and helped her to swill the yard and to shake the mats, she had completely forgotten that he had ever vexed her.

Mr Ullathorne came home about midday from the last shift of the week, had his bath in front of the fire, had his dinner, and went to sleep until nearly tea-time. Then the family set off to shop at Durham.

Kit did not go with them. He had his own plans for the evening, and they went without him. It was a mild, open evening, and there was enough daylight left for them to reach the city before the dark came down. They crossed the railway line, went down between the allotments, and passed the edge of the Fiery Heap on their way to Grey Bridge. Then they turned off, climbed the slope out of Grey Bridge, and reached the top of Observatory Hill. There below them, still clear in the slowly fading light, stood the great cathedral, immense and magnificent on its wooded peninsula. The pale grey light of the declining west was reflected in its high windows, and around it drifted the evening smoke of the packed and crooked city.

At the foot of the Observatory fields, where a path led down to the river and over the bridge, there stood a little house that Dick was very fond of. It was a little sandstone lodge, with a white door, white window-boxes and two rather ornate chimney-stacks. A white gate guarded the road to the bridge, and behind the cottage soared the great smooth beech-trees that lined the banks of the river. It was Dick's favourite house.

'Wouldn't it be champion if we lived here, Da!' he said.

'What, in that? I wouldn't take a fortune and live in that.'

'Why not?'

'Why, how could a fellow get to the pit from here? This is the back o'beyond.'

'You needn't stay in the pit for ever.'

'I wouldn't be much good for anything else.'

'You could be a lodge-keeper.'

'What, and live without any neighbours? It would give your mother the creeps to be fastened up here all by herself.'

'I don't know about that,' said Mrs Ullathorne. 'But what I do know is that if you two don't get a move on and stop staring into other folks' windows, all the shops will be shut before we get there.'

So they hurried on across the bridge, through the draughty little opening called Windy Gap, and out on to the Palace Green, the great open space between the castle and the cathedral.

This was a route that Mr Ullathorne and his wife rarely chose. Indeed, in the presence of these imposing buildings, alien and unfamiliar, they felt uneasy, and even a little guilty. They had never been inside the cathedral; they had never even peeped through the gateway to the castle. All this was to them forbidden, almost enemy territory, to be hurried through. Dick on the other hand always felt a thrill of pleasure as he came out of Windy Gap, and saw the massive old buildings enclosing the Green, the hexagon of turf with its single tree, and, in the far corner, a single yellow gas-light shining out of the shadows like a star. He felt an intense curiosity about these noble and ancient

23

houses, and a desire to venture into the alleys or vennels that ran between them. But these were feelings that his father did not share. With the air of a man marching his company across a strip of hostile territory, he crossed the Green without looking either to right or to left, hurried down Owen Gate and into the market-place.

To come upon the market-place after crossing Palace Green was like emerging from night into day, or like stepping from the pit cage at the top of the shaft; for all the shops threw their brilliant yellow light inwards upon the wide cobbled square, where the statue of the Duke on his horse rode high above the throng of traps, wagons and stalls. The stalls of the Cheap Jacks were ranged on every side of the square, and the naphtha flares swinging from the cross-beams hissed and flung their smoky flames out into the darkness, illuminating piles of pit shirts and pit jackets, pit bottles, pick-shafts, shovel handles, joints of meat and chains of sausages, rolls of oil-cloth, brushes and brooms, cups and saucers and china dogs. One man was selling patent medicines, a second sat patiently beside a pile of bird-cages containing canaries, a third was challenging bystanders to bind him and tie him in a sack, and a fourth with a huge brass weighing-machine was promising a reward to all whose weight he failed to guess correctly; but over them all could be heard the cheerful, irrepressible voice of the pot-man as he banged his wares on an up-turned tea-chest, and clanged his plates together like cymbals.

'Now then, ladies and gentlemen, here's a lovely set! Half a dozen of the best English egg-cups, specially made to fit the size of eggs laid in this city. I'll let you have them for a shilling . . . for elevenpence . . . for tenpence . . . here you are, then, ninepence the lot, ninepence the set! Nobody want them? Nobody make me an offer for these lovely egg-cups? Right, then, we'll keep them. Yes, I'll keep them for my birthday. These will be just the thing for my mantelpiece. Now what have we? Ah, now, just take a look at this lovely tea-pot, ladies. You'll never see another like this, no, not in all your born days. Here it is, made by Benjamin Telder, one of the best firms that ever sent a pot out of Staffordshire. Look at it, ladies. Just smell the flowers on that pot – hand-picked this very morning. And I'm not asking you eighteenpence . . . I'm not asking you one and three . . . here you are . . . a shilling and it's yours! A lady over there . . . and another . . . and another. Now we're doing well. My, my, we are doing well . . .'

They could have stood all night listening to the potman and his wonderful jokes, but there was shopping to be done. By the time they had done, the stall-holders were beginning to pack their wares into their traps and wagons, and the public houses were growing noisy. It was time for them to be going home, and when they came to the bottom of the long winding 'peth' that led out of the city towards Branton, they found Alfy Barnes polishing the reflectors on the lamps of his trap and waiting for customers for the last trip home.

'Room for three little 'uns, Alfy?' asked Mr Ullathorne.

'You're just in time, Davy. I was thinking of packing in for the night. Is that your Dicky? Jump in, lad, beside your mother and take the reins. Your da and me will walk up the path.'

The men footed it up the long slope out of the city, and Dick held the reins. There was little for him to do, for the horse knew its way as well as the men, but he felt proud to be in charge of the trap. It was dark now, and a wind was beginning to send clouds scudding across the sky. Looking up, Dick saw the moon ducking in and out of the clouds, and seeming to race from one to the other with a furious speed. In places great trees over-arched the narrow road, and when the moon was in, all Dick could see clearly was the heaving haunches of the horse. When they came to Nevilles Cross, and the few lights of Branton were visible across the windswept countryside, the men got in and the pony was shaken up into a trot. Nearer and nearer loomed the Fiery Heap, and at last they were at Alfy's stable, and their own street was upon them. In a few minutes they were at home, where Kit had a big fire roaring up the chimney and the kettle singing on the hob.

3

The Staple

Before they went to sleep the boys had another confab.

'Do you know where I've been this time, kidder?'

'No.'

'I've been inside the staple.'

'The staple? Where's that?'

'It's up past Albert Johnson's farm.'

'That little thing in the wood? There's nothing in there, is there?'

'There is.'

'Anyhow, it's locked, isn't it?'

'Aye, but I can get in. Have a look at this.'

Kit got up, kneed his way across the bed, took something out of his jacket pocket, and put it in Dick's hands.

'What is it?'

'It's a screw-driver.'

'Where did you get that?'

'I found it on the Fiery Heap and I scraped the rust off.'

'But you cannot get into the staple with a screw-driver.'

'I can. I took all the screws out of the hinges.'

'What's it like inside, Kit?'

'It's all queer iron ladders.'

'How many?'

'Oh I haven't counted them yet.'

The bed creaked as he crawled back to return the screw-driver to his jacket, and in the darkness Kit misjudged where he was and fell with a thump on the attic floor. They both burst out laughing and couldn't stop themselves. Then the door at the bottom of the stairs opened. It always made a peculiar sound, as if it had stuck to the frame and had to be wrenched open.

'For heaven's sake, get to sleep up there!' cried their mother. 'There's never a minute's peace with you two in the house.'

'We're just going, Ma,' cried Dick.

'Then don't forget. Every night that God sends I have to shout up to you two lads.'

'We'll pinch a bit of candle,' whispered Kit when he heard the stair door close, 'and we'll make a proper lamp, and then we'll have a good look at the ladders. What do you say, kidder?'

Kit's wonderful plans seemed exciting enough by day. Put in a secret whisper, in the dark of the stuffy little attic, with no one to overhear, they were irresistible. Before Dick fell asleep he had agreed to everything.

The next day was Sunday, and although neither of the boys went to chapel they were made to put on their best clothes. Both of them wore heavy grey knickerbockers and belted jackets, and Dick had to suffer a starched collar that chafed his neck. Nevertheless, Sunday clothes or no Sunday clothes, Kit was bent on taking another look at the staple, and they set off after breakfast. They had to trespass to get to it, first through Albert Johnson's farm and then for half a mile along the railway line that led up to the fells; but Kit had spied out the land, and knew that both the farm and the line would be deserted. Half an hour after leaving home they were in the little wood where the staple entrance stood.

This staple, which was a footway down to underground workings, was something of a mystery. No one knew when it had been made. Those who knew about it thought that it was the entrance to the old pit that had been worked before the big shaft had been sunk at Branton, but there was no one in the colliery who could remember its being used. Many years ago a rough brick hut had been built over the entrance, and bushes and quick-growing sycamores had almost overgrown the hut. The tarred and pitched door was locked in three places, and the locks were all rusted.

Kit did not bother with them. He quickly unscrewed the hinges from the frame, taking care to put the screws where he could easily find them again, and pulled the door away. The boys stepped inside and found themselves standing on a rusty iron grid, from which a flight of metal rungs dropped and disappeared into the darkness.

Dick was overawed by the blackness and the danger.

'You're not going down there, are you?'

'I am. What do you think I've come for?'

'With your best clothes on?'

'They won't spoil.'

'How deep is it?'

'That's what I'm ganna find out.'

'But we haven't a lamp, Kit.'

'Makes no odds. Just keep a look-out and see if anybody's coming.'

He set off down the ladder and Dick watched him with horror. First his legs disappeared and then his back, then his shoulders and head, and finally his fingers. The ladder looked very steep, and Dick's hair bristled when he thought of what might lie below. Everything seemed to grow very silent. All he could hear was the sound of his brother's boots as they scraped on the rungs, and even this sound grew fainter and fainter till it was almost inaudible. From beyond the door he heard a buzzer sounding from another colliery. Then there was a startling clatter of wings as a pigeon broke cover and flew out of the wood. The danger, the loneliness, the fear of sudden discovery – all these made his heart beat fast; but a few moments later he heard his brother ascending, saw his fingers, his arms and then his head appear.

'What's it like, Kit?'

'It's champion. There's no end to these ladders. You go down one ladder and come to a little platform. There's another flight after that, and then another platform. It seems to go on for ever.'

'How many did you go down?'

'Five, I think.'

'Five!'

'That's nothing. We'll have to make a lamp, Dick, and then we'll get to the bottom.'

'What, now?'

'Nay, not now,' replied Kit. 'We have nothing here to make a muggie with. But I'll not rest till I see what's at the bottom.'

'It's daftness without a muggie, Kit.'

'I know it's daftness. But what about trying one or two ladders now?'

'Who, me?'

'Aye.'

'Now, with my Sunday clothes on?'

'Aye.'

'I daren't, Kit.'

'Don't be so soft. Try just one.'

'How far is it down?'

'It's no distance. Look, you can see the first platform from here.'

Dick looked down but could see nothing. After the first few rungs everything was pitch black. Kit threw a pebble down. It rattled on the first platform and bounced down with a daunting, disappearing sound. Dick was terrified, but he was even more afraid of appearing a coward in the eyes of his brother. He began to descend, his hands trembling and gripping the iron rungs as if he meant to bend them. After about a dozen faltering downward steps he found himself on the first platform. Looking up he could see the light coming in through the staple door, and his brother's body bending over him. He had the feeling that he was standing on nothing but a column of black air that might give way and part beneath him if he moved.

'I'm coming up now, Kit.'

'Already?'

'Yes.'

'Come on then. Up you come . . . well done, kidder!'

Back at the top, warmed by his brother's approval, and safe, Dick felt relieved, excited, even proud.

'Kit, it was good,' he said, as the hinges were being put back into place. 'And we're not very dirty, are we?'

They dusted each other, slapping each other hard in their excitement, and all the way home they talked about their plans for getting lamps and food, for making a deeper descent, for embarking on a real exploration.

4

A Sick Man

The next day Kit went back to school and was caned, as
Mr Allcroft had threatened. Dick saw him come through
the door in the partition blowing on his hands. The cane
had hurt him but he was too much of a man to show it.

Kit was a born rebel. He rebelled not out of awkward-
ness or malice or principle, but by nature. His father could
have withdrawn him from school, but he kept him there
hoping to give him some show of an education. He knew
that both his boys would, in all likelihood, end up by
working in the pit, but he did not want them to miss any
other chances that might come their way for lack of training. Kit, like Dick, was not without brains, but he hated
lessons. He was happiest when he was using his hands,
helping the boilerman, repairing broken desks, making the
ink. He could not bear to be chained to a desk, and every
now and then he would go off with any dealer, any rag-
and-bone man, hawker or vagabond who would take him.
No amount of punishment would keep him at home, and
his father had long since given up the attempt to tame him.

He was a big boy for his age, and though his mother
tried to get him to wear schoolboy knickerbockers, he
really liked to dress like a pitman, with his cloth cap pulled
well over to one side of his head, his waistcoat open, and
a thin white scarf knotted round his neck, and pulled to

one side. He kept his hair cropped close, except for a 'topping' which stuck out just over his forehead. He was tough and fearless, but completely without malice. He was secretly the apple of his father's eye, and to Dick everything he did was wonderful.

For the next few days bad weather kept him away from the staple or any other mischief that he might have had in mind.

He did not buy a greyhound, but instead he brought home two racing pigeons. He kept them for a day or two in a loft belonging to Bobby Keegan's father who lived only a few doors away; but he was a handy lad and quickly knocked up a 'cree' for his birds on the waste land at the front of the house; and once he had 'hanted' them, as he called it, that is, accustomed them to their new home, he began to fly them. It was not easy to provide enough exercise for them, but every week-end he and Dick would take them as far away from the colliery as they could, and then release them. Kit taught his brother how to handle the birds, and how to launch them into the air. It was wonderful to see them climb and circle and then make off for home.

One Saturday Kit could not take his pigeons away, and he asked Dick if he would go on his own to Broomilaw and release them there. Dick had never been right into Broomilaw. He knew where it was. Part of it was visible from Branton, and from the end of Chapel Row you could see the nearest houses appearing over the horizon, the stocks and pulleys, and the conical tip of the slag heap. The colliery was no more than four miles away, but it was the last place that Dick wanted to visit. He had heard queer tales about the Broomilaw boys. They did not like strangers, and at school he had heard stories about boys being pelted out of the place with stones, and about a way they had there of punching you in the middle so that it winded you. However, it was enough for him that Kit wanted him to go; Kit's word was law. Besides, he knew that he was not expected to go right into the colliery; it would be enough to get somewhere near it. He took two brown paper bags, pinched air holes into them, put the birds inside, and set off.

He knew most of the way. He had to go past the school, over the fields past the Fiery Heap, cross the narrow road that connected Durham with the remote collieries farther up the valley of the Deerness, then go over the Deerness itself and up the long slope to Broomilaw. He had done part of the journey before. Not far from the point where he had to cut across the road there was a dark little farm with a deaf and dumb farmhand who sometimes made weird and fearsome noises at you as you went past; and one day he had been dared to swim in the Deerness, and had nearly fallen into a sheephole, and had come out with queer spots like tar on his shoulders and arms.

He crossed the rickety bridge over the river, rocking it to see how shaky it was, and then went cautiously on towards Broomilaw. It seemed very quiet in the colliery, but after he had released his pigeons and the sound of their wings had died away, he heard the slapping of a ball up against a wall; and moving slowly and quietly along in the shelter of the allotment fence he saw that some men were playing hand-ball. The end wall of one of the colliery rows had been enlarged to make a ball-alley, and around the bare, flat patch of earth that made the foreground

34

about forty men were quietly watching and playing. The players were stripped to the waist, and Dick could see that they were miners by the square of coal dirt down their backs. The players were hot, and the sweat made little white channels as it ran down their backs. The spectators seemed friendly and good-humoured. Dick edged little by little towards them, and soon mingled with the crowd.

It was Saturday afternoon. The pulley wheels were idle and the men were prepared to enjoy their sport. As the grey day darkened, more and more players came forward to keep the game going. The twilight echoed with the pad of the ball against the palm, and the sharper smack as it hit the bare wall. Branton possessed no alley like Broomilaw's, and Dick stayed on, pleased not to be molested, and enjoying the game. The players did not stop until it was almost too dark to see.

It was very dark when Dick turned to go home. He was not afraid. The darkness held few terrors for the Branton boys who played every night up and down the dark streets. He found his way easily down the slope, crossed the bridge and came to the road.

He was just crossing it when to his surprise he saw two red lights moving and stopping about fifty yards away from him. He stopped and watched them, and made them out to be the rear glasses of two trap-lamps, and, going forward very cautiously, he saw what looked like an empty trap with a black pony in the shafts. The pony was cropping the rough grass on the verge of the road and was pulling the trap's nearside wheel dangerously near the ditch. There was no sound except the jingling of the bit as the pony grazed, and the creaking of the trap as it was

dragged forward. Dick drew near with great caution, and
then, still seeing no one at hand, he took the pony by the
bit and pulled it back on to the road.

'Come up, lad!' he said, and almost jumped out of his
skin when a voice answered him from the trap.

'Who's that?'
'It's me.'
'Man or a boy?'
'A boy.'
'Come and give me a hand, boy.'

37

Dick dropped the bit and going round to the back of the trap he saw a man sitting on the floor with his head on the seat-cushion.

'What's the matter, mister?'

'I can't get up.'

'Are you hurt?'

'It's a pain, here, just under the heart I can't sit up properly.'

'The trap was nearly in the ditch. That's why I moved it.'

'Do you think you can drive this trap?'

'I don't think so.'

'Can you lead the pony?'

'Yes, I can do that.'

'Can you take me nearly into Durham?'

'There's a farm just close by.'

Dick no sooner mentioned the farm than he remembered the deaf and dumb hand that frightened him. He was relieved when the man said:

'No, I want to get home. I'll be all right there.'

'Will you tell me the way?'

'Yes, but get started. Go down this road till you get to Grey Bridge, and then I'll tell you where to go next.'

Dick began to lead the pony away. He began to run but the man called out to him not to trot the pony. He could not stand the jolting of the trap, so Dick went on gently but as quickly as he could till he came to Grey Bridge. There they turned off the main road into the city and went over Barn Hill down towards the Butty Fields. At every turning the man gave directions, but after a while they were unnecessary, for the pony seemed to know it was near home and took the turnings of its own accord.

At last they turned into a dark drive with black bushes growing thickly on either side. The wheels of the trap crunched over an uneven cindery surface, and the trap-lamps shone weakly on the dark-leaved rhododendrons. At the end of the drive rose an ugly rectangular house with a big blank doorway painted a dull brown and fringed with grubby ivy. Not a single light was visible.

'Have I to knock on the door?' asked Dick.

'No. There's a handle there on the right-hand side. Pull it.'

Dick felt around for a moment and then his hand found a bell-pull with a rusty, damp feel to it. He tugged it and from somewhere in the back of the house came the jangling of a bell. No one answered it. He had to pull again, and again, before a wavering light appeared, and heavy steps were heard approaching. Then the door was wrenched open and an old man appeared with a lantern.

'What is it?' he asked.

'It's a man in the trap. He's ill. He's bad.'

'What?' said the old man, cupping his ear with his hand.

'It's me, you fat-head!' said the man in the trap.

'What?'

'Me!'

Realizing that the old man was too hard of hearing ever to understand what was said, Dick took the lantern from his hand and shone it into the trap.

'Bliss my sowl! It's Mr Sleath. What's come over him?'

'He can't walk.'

'What, is he took bad again? Dinna worry, Mr Sleath, we'll soon have you in bed.'

To Dick's surprise the old man took hold of Mr Sleath, edged him towards the door of the trap, then picked him up bodily and carried him upstairs, with Dick going before him with the lantern. They went into a room that was a kind of office. There the servant lowered the sick man into a chair, lit more candles, and told Dick to get downstairs and keep an eye on the pony. Dick found that it had moved away a bit and was trying to crop the thin turf of the lawn. He took hold of the bit and stood there, with nothing to look at but the grey starless sky, the black humped forms of the bushes and the cold bare hall of the house with its big stained flagstones and dull brown walls. It was chilly waiting there and he thought the old man would never reappear. Eventually however he did come down.

'Is Mr Sleath better?'

'What?'

'Is Mr Sleath all right now?'

'Yes, yes, not sae bad. Here's something for you. Here, take it,' (passing a florin to him). 'Have you far to walk?'

'Just to Branton.'

'Where?'

'Branton.'

'Better make tracks, my bonny lad, and I'll put the pony in the stable. Off tha gans. Hop it, and dinna lose that two-bob bit.'

It was very late when Dick got home. His father had worked himself up into a bad temper at his non-appearance, but his frowns vanished when Dick told them all the adventures of the night.

'And did you find out what this gentleman's name was?' asked Mr Ullathorne when Dick had come to the end of his story.

'The servant called him Mr Sleath or something like that.'

'Mr Sleath! Was he a shortish fellow with a dark face?'

'As far as I could see, Da.'

'Ye beggar of Hexham! You've been in good company, lad. Do you know who this chap is?'

'No, Da.'

'He's the boss! Man alive, he's the man that owns all Branton. Haven't you seen "Sleath and Partners" on the wagons?'

'Is he the same man?'

'The identical fellow! Blow me, lad, I don't want to wish him any harm but the worse he is the better for all of us here.'

'Why's that, Da?'

'Lad, he's just about the worst master that ever walked the face of this earth. I'll not break my heart if he never gets up again. Did you tell him your name?'

'Nobody asked me that.'

'Makes no odds. I'd rather not be beholden to a chap like that.'

Dick could not quite understand why his father felt so strongly about Mr Sleath. He had spoken a little roughly, but he had been in pain. Besides he had given him a florin, and that was more than he had ever been given before in all his life. He was so puzzled that he forgot to ask if the pigeons had got home safely.

5

The Affair of the Backshift Overman

About ten days or so later the boys were coming home from school, kicking a tin along the gutters, when Kit's sharp senses began to tell him that there was something unusual in the air. When they turned into Chapel Row, they could see all the women out at their yard gates, all their heads turned towards the pithead.

'What's up, Mrs Keegan?' asked Kit.

'Nobody seems to know, but there's some talk about a cage stuck half-way up the shaft.'

'Anybody in it?'

'They say it's full of men coming up from the backshift.'

'Come on, Dicky, let's have a look.'

When the boys reached the pit yard they saw forty or fifty men gathered there, and a scattering of women. The pulley wheels were at a standstill, and no sound came out of the winding-engine room. The men were obviously in an ugly frame of mind. Some of them had picked up stones and lengths of timber, and Dick saw one man with a rusty horseshoe in his hand. As the boys pushed forward they were angrily motioned back.

'Get them lads out of the way before they get hurt,' someone said, but the men were too concerned with their own affairs to see that the boys were removed. Dick and

Kit hung around on the fringe of the crowd, listening to the men and asking questions of the women; and they picked up the information that for some reason or other the cage was being held half-way up the shaft.

There had been some trouble underground but nobody seemed to know what.

There was a lull, then the men began to stir, and one of them went over to the door of the engine-room, and began to hammer on it with his stick.

'Sam!' he cried. 'Are you there, Sam?'

'Aye.'

It was hard to catch Sam's voice because all the doors and windows were closed.

'What are ye up to, Sam? D'ye not realize there's a cage

44

full of men stuck fast in the shaft?'

Sam came to the window and called through it without opening it.

'I have orders to keep them there.'

'Whose orders?'

'Backshift Overman.'

When they heard the Overman mentioned the men began to stir and grow restless.

'Sam!'

'Aye.'

'Get them men up!'

'I daren't.'

' I warn ye, Sam. We'll break the door down and we'll bring them up ourselves.'

'You'll make me lose my job.'

'You'll be in good company,' shouted one of the men, and a stone went smash through one of the windows. 'That's a warning, Sam. We're coming in.'

Another stone went through a window, and the men began to shout. They hammered on the door, then paused once more to see what Sam was going to do. At length he was heard again.

'All right, I'll lift them. Leave me alone, and I'll fetch them up for you.'

Sam's face was withdrawn from the window, and all eyes were turned upon the pulley wheels. After a short delay they began to turn, and the greasy rope began to fly upwards. A few seconds later the 'butterfly' appeared, the cage itself rose and sank back upon the 'keps', the little metal shoulders that held it in position, and the doors were pushed open. Five men were crouching in the cage, and a sixth was lying on the floor. They were all black with pit dirt, but the sweat was running down their faces. The men carried their sick companion out and laid him on the ground.

Kit began to push forward and Dick edged after him, but just at that moment their father came into the yard.

'Trust you two to be where you aren't wanted! Now, get home, the pair of ye! This is no place for lads. Jossy, Flem, get all these lads out of the way.'

All the boys were turned away, and Kit and Dick to their great disappointment had to go home. Within a few minutes however they knew as much as if they had stayed, for the story of the Backshift Overman had spread like wildfire. He had had an argument with some of the men at the face, and out of spite had stopped the cage in the

46

shaft, just opposite a vent where bad air was coming out. It had been a spiteful and dangerous thing to do, and all the colliery was burning with resentment. Kit could see that his father, for one, was not going to take the affair lying down.

He kept his eye on his father that night. Mr Ullathorne was quiet but restless. He kept looking at the clock and poking the fire. Once he went over to the cupboard and drew a pair of pit stockings over his hands as though he was looking for holes. He seemed anxious to get the boys off to bed. They delayed as long as they could, and when they were finally driven upstairs Kit did not undress, but kept everything on except his boots, and left the door of the attic slightly ajar, so that he could hear what was happening downstairs.

'What's the matter, Kit? Why don't you get into bed?'

'Whisht! I'm waiting to see what happens.'

'What do you mean?'

'I think there's something in the wind. I think my da is going out somewhere.'

They listened and they heard their mother preparing for bed, filling the kettle and moving the fire-irons back from the fire.

'Aye, get to bed, Hetty,' Kit could hear his father say. 'I'm just popping out for a minute.'

'At this time of the night? What on earth for?'

'I just want to have a word with Flem Fairless.'

'It's a bit late, isn't it, to be knocking on people's doors?'

'I said I would meet him just outside the Institute.'

'It seems to me as if the lot of you are up to some monkey business.'

'It's nothing to worry about. Just get into bed, Hetty.'

47

Kit gently closed the door and withdrew as he heard his mother coming to bed. Then he pushed open the skylight till it had folded completely open, took up his boots and handed them to Dick.

'What are you doing this for?'

'I'm going out.'

'They'll hear you.'

'I'm going out through here.' He pointed to the skylight.

'Can I come with you, Kit?'

'Not this time, kidder.'

'Why not?'

'I want you to listen in case my mother gets suspicious. Listen!'

'Kit, I'm coming as well. Wait till I get my things on.'

'Dinna be daft. We'll get caught.'

'We won't. If you're going I am.'

'Come on then.'

They heard the downstairs door open and shut again, and then their father's footsteps going across the yard. As soon as he felt sure he would not be detected Kit wriggled through the skylight, hung his boots around his neck, slid down the slates and dropped lightly on to the top of the wash-house. He caught Dick as he slid after him, and then they both set off to follow their father.

He did not go to the Institute. Instead he waited near the coal depots until he was joined by about five or six others. The boys could not hear what they were saying but thought they could see them drawing things over their hands and faces. Then another figure appeared hurrying through the dark from the direction of the colliery offices and whistled softly. Immediately they all moved off together towards the colliery pond.

6

Revenge

Mr Sleath who, if not the sole owner of Branton, was the largest shareholder and managing-director, was a man of very regular habits. The house in which he lived and to which Dick had taken him on the night of his illness stood in its own grounds just outside the city of Durham. Mr Sleath had made money out of coal and had bought the house a few years ago; and since he was of a pious turn of mind he had altered the name to Sion House. He had an interest in several collieries but Branton was his chief concern, and every Monday, Wednesday, and Friday he drove from the city to Branton to interview his manager and his three overmen. On those evenings he expected to be given a full report on the workings of the pit, and he did not mind how long he stayed.

On this particular evening he had come to see the Backshift Overman, the man who had been responsible for holding up the cage. Mr Wanless was a large man with a raw complexion, as if he had a kind of shaving rash. The interview took place in a little room in the colliery office building.

'Now, Wanless,' said Mr Sleath, 'I want to get to the bottom of this affair. And I may as well say that I consider it very important, because I intend to stamp out this sort of behaviour right at the very beginning. So tell me everything. When did it start?'

'Just this morning, Mr Sleath.'

'And where?'

'In the Low Main.'

'And what was the cause of the trouble? Now, be precise, Wanless.'

'Well, I was of the opinion that these men were getting careless, Mr Sleath. I've told them time and time again that they're filling too much stone in the tubs. So I said that I would start laying out the tubs if they were not careful. That set them off. They all started saying that the stone should be sorted out properly, and I should give them the weight for the coal that was left. But I told them that wasn't in the regulations. "If a tub is under-weight," I said, "you know as well as me that I canna credit you with it, and I winna credit you with it. You can put that in your pipes and smoke it," I said.'

'You were perfectly right.'

'I knew I was right, but you should have heard the grumbling I had to put up with. "You want this, and you want that," I said to them. "You'll be asking for the pit next." Then one of them said, "We just want our rights, and we'll see that we get them."'

'Who was that?'

'I think it was Jo Tredennick.'

'Are you sure?'

'I cannot be positive, Mr Sleath, but if it wasn't him it was one of the others.'

'Yes, yes, that's obvious. But try not to give vague answers. Before I decide on any action, I want to be sure of my facts.'

'Anyhow, I lost my temper with the lot of them. I got on to the winding-engine man and I told him to stop the cage in the shaft, just to teach the beggars a lesson.'

'And did he obey you?'

'He did at first. But the folks in the colliery got to hear about it, and they came to the pithead and made a scene. There was that much bad feeling, that the engine-man got frightened and lifted the men without waiting for more orders.'

'What's this man's name?'

'Sammy Pybus.'

'Is there anybody that can take his place?'

'Any amount. There's two or three that would jump at the job.'

'Trained men?'

'Yes, Mr Sleath.'

'Then tell Mr Curtiss that this man Pybus is to get his notice.'

'Yes, Mr Sleath.'

'And I want a list of all those men in the Low Main who were troublesome. I'll be in for it tomorrow.'

'Yes, Mr Sleath.'

'Right, that'll do for tonight.'

Wanless sighed with relief. He had had a trying day – an argument at the coal-face, a scene at the pithead, a long shift, and then a weary interview with Mr Sleath. He was pleased when 'the boss' finished making his check of all the doors and cupboards and drawers in the office and climbed into his trap.

It was by now nearing midnight. All the machinery of the mine was still awake. The cage rose, fell back on the safety 'keps', was released, fell and rose again. The pulley wheels spun quickly now this way, now that. There was a noise of shunting from the sidings, and occasional hammerings from the shops. In the great wooden condenser the hot water steamed and dripped. Yet there was no one to be seen. The pit yard was deserted, and the streets beyond it were empty.

Mr Wanless lived in Church Street, a superior row with high-walled yards, where most of the officials lived. The way there led first of all across a piece of open land where on one side rose a large Methodist Chapel, and on the other a tarry fish-and-chip shed leaned against a telegraph pole; and then it ran alongside the colliery pond. The pond was a biggish reservoir, a collecting basin for water pumped out of the pit, and a resting place for all the unwanted things of the colliery – old prams, pails, mangles, and kittens. It had once been fenced in but now the railings were broken, and it was easy to get to the edge of the water.

It was here by the edge of the pond that the men were lying in wait. No one who did not know they were there could have spotted them. They had pulled black stockings over their arms and dark-coloured bags over their faces. They were perfectly silent and perfectly still. It was safe to say that only two people knew they were there. They were Kit and Dick, who had followed them from the depots, and were now hidden behind the big pipes that fed the water into the pond.

There was no one else about. The Overman came slowly along the path, leaning heavily upon his stick. The stick was barely visible in the darkness, but on the shiny leather of his helmet glowed the reflection of a distant street-lamp. As he drew near to the ambush he stooped to fasten a loose bootlace, and in an instant something was thrown over his head, he was lifted clean off his feet, and flung

like a log out into the cold and dirty waters of the pond. Almost before the body had risen for the first time to the surface, his assailants had melted into the night. There had been no witnesses to the deed but the men who had done it – and Kit and Dick.

'Come on, Dick,' whispered Kit. 'If we don't get back first there'll be ructions.'

'No. We can't go yet. He might drown!'

'What – he's that fat he'll float like a football. Look – there he is, climbing out already.'

They watched the Overman trying to climb up the sloping stonework that edged the pond, and heard him curse as he slipped and went back into the water. Once he had got out they did not dare to stir until he had moved away. Only when they saw him standing under the street-light and shaking himself did they emerge from their hiding-place.

'Come on,' said Kit, but Dick stood irresolutely looking at the retreating figure. The quickness of the deed had stunned him. He had not known that his father could do things like this; he did not know whether to look on him as wicked or wonderfully brave.

When they got home they found that their father had beaten them there, and they had to wait outside until they saw the kitchen light go out. They gave their father a few minutes to get to sleep, then climbed on to the wash-house, crept over the slates and got in through the sky-light. They listened carefully, but he was already sleeping the sleep of those whose conscience is good.

The next day the story of the ducking of the Overman was all over the colliery, and there was hardly a house that did not have a good laugh at his expense, but so well concealed was the identity of the men who had ducked him that no one except Kit and Dick knew who had done the deed. Mr Sleath was furious at the news. He was infuriated that one of his servants had been the victim of such a practical joke; but his anger almost crossed the bounds of sanity when he discovered that, try as he might, he could not find out the names of the culprits.

It was, of course, the men who had been kept in the cage who were the first to come under suspicion; but each one had a dozen witnesses to prove that he had never been near the pond at the time of the ducking. Every minute of the day Dick expected the police to turn their attention to him, and whenever he saw a 'bobby' he felt paralysed with guilt and fear, and wondered what he would say if he was questioned. But no one came. No one seemed to think of connecting the Ullathornes with the affair; and Mr Ulla-thorne himself was so inscrutable that Dick sometimes wondered if after all his father had really been there.

Soon the police had to confess that they could get no further with the affair. To Mr Sleath's annoyance they dropped their inquiries and advised him to give up the prosecution. He had no option but to follow their advice. He abandoned the case, but his resentment against the men who had defied him did not die down. He nursed his grievance and waited for an opportunity to revenge himself upon them.

7

The Staple Again

While the affair of the Overman was being talked about
the boys were busy preparing for the second descent of
the staple. Kit still had some of the money he had earned
at Towin Law, and with it he bought three good candles,
out of which he made six lights. Then after days of rum-
maging on the Fiery Heap they found the framework of
two lanterns, one a good stout trap-lamp with no handle,
and the other an old-fashioned pit-lamp that had lost its
heat-shield. They both gave a decent light but the first
was awkward to handle, and the other grew too hot to the
fingers. Kit mended them both, stole a box of matches
from the cupboard, and hid all his equipment inside the
staple hut.

For the next few days it rained, and there was no possibility of making the trip, but towards the end of the week
the weather cleared, and news came of an unexpected holiday. On Friday the whole school was to be used as a polling
booth, and every class had a holiday. Besides, it was 'baff'
Friday, a day on which the pay was not to be collected.
The boys had the whole day at their disposal.

Friday was always a busy day for the women of the
colliery, for it was then that the cleaning of the week came
to its climax. Almost every hour of the day was given over
to some task – black-leading the great shining kitchen

range, scouring and whitening the hearth, cleaning the
knives with emery-paper, scrubbing the floors, and polishing the complicated fire-irons, fender, tidy, and tongs.
Mrs Ullathorne was not altogether sorry when she heard
that her boys wanted to go on the fells for the day. Friday
was not a day on which she wished to have two idle boys
hanging about the house; the work could be best done
when they were out of the way. She gave them some bread
and cheese, and a bottle of homemade ginger beer, and
did not ask too many questions about their intentions.

'By, them two lads are a blessing to you, Hetty,' said her
neighbour. 'I've just seen them going up the street together,
and I thought to myself what a couple of nice lads they
were. Now there's my two – woman, they're forever in
the house. I have to step over them like a clocker over her

chickens. And talk about fighting – they're at it from morning till night. It's something chronic.'

'You needn't think that mine's models, Mary Jane,' replied Hetty. 'They'll be up to some mischief or other, I bet. Especially our Kit. He's the plague of our life, is that one. But I will say that he's never been one for cluttering up the house.'

'Surely he'll not stray very far when he has your little Dicky with him.'

'I hope not. But to tell the truth, I'm past worrying, Mary Jane. Give us a hand to shake these mats, will you?'

It was a fine day, one of those days that come unexpectedly in winter, when one can hardly believe the calendar. The streets were black and miry, but there was a hint of greenness in the clumps of wild barley grass that grew in the few untrodden corners. The starlings on the slatey roofs were swooping excitedly from chimney to chimney, giving long penetrating whistles, and in the field beyond the fish shop at the end of the street a single lark could be heard singing and climbing into the mild air. In the streets the sheets and shirts of the late launderers – most of the women liked to finish their washing early in the week – flapped and swung as the west wind blew gently in from the fell.

The two boys had to make a long detour to get to the staple without being detected. They turned at the top of the street as if they were making for the fells, climbed for about half a mile, and then worked their way along the lee of a rough hawthorn hedge, and through a patch of gorse until they were once more in sight of the railway line. The tankie was coming up the line, making for the fell drifts, labouring and straining in front of its five trucks. It was going so slowly that the tender-man, who had jumped down and was testing the couplings with his long pole, could keep up with it on foot, and the boys could easily read the white lettering on the soiled side of each wagon –

SLEATH AND PARTNERS
RETURN TO BRANTON COLLIERY

They let the tankie pass, and did not emerge from the gorse until it had struggled round the bend and was out of sight. Then they ran across the line like partridges, crept along a bramble hedge, and came at last to the little wood where the staple was sited.

It was obvious that no one but Kit had been there. There were no new marks on the mud outside, and the lock and hinges were untouched. The screw-driver was where Kit always left it, wrapped in a piece of oily cloth and stuffed up a hollow in the root of one of the sycamores.

It did not take them long to make sure that they were not being watched, to remove the hinges, and slew the door open. They left the ginger beer inside the hut, but Kit tied a pit bottle containing water round his neck. Then he stowed all the food away into his pockets, lit the lamps and pulled the door back into position.

Dick had not foreseen the last of these preparations, and the closing of the door robbed him immediately of his courage. He had assumed that they would have the help of daylight for the first few flights. He had vaguely imagined that the light coming through the door would remain visible all the way, like the friendly mouth of a cave; but suddenly it was so dark that he could not see even the first ladder.

Slowly however his eyes grew accustomed to the darkness, and he began to make out the lines of the grid on which they stood. The opening took shape, and then the ladder descending almost vertically. Kit, who seemed to have no nerves, was ready to descend. He carried the lamp in his left hand, and gripped the ladder with his right. Dick's lantern shone on his face, and it looked like the face of a man who is about to drown and to be sucked down into the depths of a dark river. After one quick smile the face was pulled under, feet clanged on the next grid, and it was Dick's turn to follow.

The descent was far harder than it had been before. On the first occasion he had not been hampered by a lamp, and had been able to go down hand over hand. Now he had only one hand to cling with. At every step he had to let go of one rung and clutch at the next, and every time he did it he felt that he was going to fall backwards. He took to wrapping his lamp arm as far as he could around the ladder to try to get a little extra support. This tactic steadied him a little, but the lamp, now held neck-high, shone gruesomely on the wet and slimy walls of the shaft as he descended.

The shaft had been only very roughly bricked in; some of the bricks had fallen out and some had mouldered away almost to nothing. The walls glistened like snail-trails. At first a few fronds with small but perfectly formed leaves grew out of the cracks and strained upwards to the light, but after he had reached the foot of the first ladder Dick saw no more plants, and the only colours his lamp revealed were the black and rust of the brickwork, and the yellow and buff of the stone where the casing had fallen away. The rungs of the ladder were rusty and rough to the touch, and he could feel the ironwork rubbing coarsely against his sleeve as he descended.

When he arrived at the first landing he looked down and saw Kit one flight below him. He was shining his lamp upwards on the hole in the grid where the next flight started. Striped shadows fell across both the boys, and Dick had the sensation of being in a strange kind of prison where it was not the walls but the floors and ceilings that were made of bars. Very cautiously he began on the second flight.

From then onwards Kit, very patiently, kept only one flight ahead of him. Now and then he called out to him to get a move on, but in the main he was very good-natured and did not shout too loudly. After six flights he began to wait for Dick to catch up with him before going on.

In this manner they proceeded until they had descended eleven flights. The walls of the staple were drier now, and they seemed sounder. Only here and there had a brick fallen out. A strange smell began to arise in the shaft, like the smell of the cupboard in which their father's pit clothes were kept; but it was still and warm, and the boys even began to sweat a little. The light from their lamps seemed if anything a little stronger. Their feet clanged strangely on the metal platforms, and their voices seemed to echo and fly upwards.

After the eleventh flight, however, Dick was made aware of a different noise, and no sooner had he heard it than Kit called out.

'I think we are getting near the bottom, kidder.'

'How do you know?'

'I'm on wood now.'

'What do you mean, Kit?'

'It's a wooden platform. Wait a bit. I can see a trapdoor and steps that look like wood. It's a sort of wooden ladder.'

Dick joined him and they both shone their lamps through the hole, but all they could make out was a ladder with wooden rungs vanishing like the others into the darkness.

'I'll try it,' said Kit, lowering himself at once.

'What's it like?'

'It's not so steep. I think it's a bit easier.'

'Is it safe?'

'Safe as houses. Come on, come down after me.'

Dick too lowered himself and began to feel his way down the wooden ladder. The angle was not so steep as before, but he had not gone down for more than a dozen rungs when something creaked and parted above him. The whole ladder gave way, fell, then hit something, broke and threw him off. Before he knew what had happened he had fallen into something soft and squelchy, and the shaft was in darkness.

'Kit! Kit!' he shouted.

'I'm here, kidder,' replied Kit, and Dick was astonished to hear his voice so close to him. 'Are you all right?'

'I've dabbed on my shoulder.'

'Is it broken?'

'I don't think so. Can you light the lamp?'

'I'll have to find it first . . . Here it is! Lad, we're lucky, and the matches are still dry.'

He struck one and set about lighting the lamp. The candle wick sizzled a bit at first, but at last it caught alight, and they could look round and take stock. They had certainly reached the bottom of the shaft, but not in the way they meant to. It was the last flight that had been the cause of the mishap. The ladder had rotted at the top, fallen against the walling and broken into several lengths. Now they were fifteen feet below the trapdoor, and with no means of climbing back to it.

It was too much for Dick. All his courage went at one ebb. His shoulder began to hurt, his trousers were sticking to his legs, he felt plastered with mud, and he was sure that they would never get out of the shaft. He began to cry.

'Don't cry, kidder,' said Kit. 'Let's have our bait.'

'I don't want anything.'

'Come on, kidder. Dinna worry. We'll get out. Come on, have a drink.'

While they were eating, Kit tried to size up the situation. There was clearly no way of getting up to the trapdoor. There were no holds in the wall as far as he could see. The largest length of ladder that had remained sound was no more than about eight feet long; but there was a tunnel leading away from the bottom of the staple. It seemed wide and dry, and the obvious thing was to explore it.

'We'll have to try this way, Dick. There might be some gear left in it somewhere. Anyhow it's bound to lead to some place. But we'll have to leave a few marks here and there just to show us the way back. What have you got in your pockets?'

'I've got a bit of string . . . and a piece of chalk.'

'Champion, lad. We'll make a mark now and then. Just one little cross about half-way up the face. What do you think about that notion, Dick?'

'I've read about explorers doing that. It's a good idea.'

Dick was feeling better already. The food had done him good, his clothes were beginning to dry on him, and it was

63

difficult to feel despondent for long when Kit was in charge.

At first the going was remarkably easy. The roof was fairly high, and Dick did not have to stoop. The bottom was fairly even, and there was only one way with no cross-roads and no side-turnings. There was no need for them to put their chalk marks on the face, but they continued to do so. After a little while, however, just after they had stopped to change candles, the going grew harder. There were sudden drops in the level of the floor, and the top began to bend and dip. The passage grew narrower, and here and there it was obstructed by falls. Old timber, broken and crushed by the movement of the earth, en-cumbered the way, and in places the gallery seemed to have been squeezed together as if the sides had been made, not of stone, but of rubber. There were dips and cracks in the floor, and in the larger hollows where water had collected they had to take off their boots and stockings. At last they came to a place where a great fall had oc-curred, and there was barely room for them to wriggle through. On the other side the way had been boarded up with very old and thick planks, green, rotting and almost phosphorescent.

It seemed as if they had come to the end. The barrier was not impassable, for the planks had in places rotted away, and the exposed nails were thin and rusty, but the outlook was not comforting. The way looked completely deserted.

Suddenly, however, Kit began to sniff.

'Sniff, kidder!' he said.

'What for?'

'Sniff hard. Can you smell anything?'

'I think I can.'

'What is it?'

'I think it's baccy.'

'So do I. Somebody's smoking.'

'They're not allowed to.'

'They can, here. I've heard my da say it's a safe pit. There's no gas here.'

'Who is it?'

'I canna tell, but he canna be far off. Come on.'

They both wriggled past the fall, levered one of the soft, pulpy planks from the barrier, went on, and then, at the end of the gallery they saw a hewer at work in his cavil. He was wearing a dirty vest, a pair of short trousers, and a little 'slush' or sludge cap to keep his head dry. He was sitting on a little stool or cracket, swinging his pick and levering the coal away from the face. The blue smoke from his pipe was lying in thin horizontal layers against the roof of the seam.

'There now, Dick, I knew we'd find a way out,' said Kit.

'Yes, but dare we go that way?'

'Not without being seen.'

'Even if we did get past him, we couldn't get up the shaft, could we?'

'Wait a bit, Dick. I think he's heard somebody. There's somebody shouting for him.'

A voice was heard farther away down the gallery calling 'Jossie! Jossie!' and in response the man laid down his pick and went off.

'Did you see what he did, Dick? He left his pick.'

'What does that matter?'

'If we had a pick, I think I could make holes in the side of the staple, the way men do when they're climbing on ice. Then we could get back on to the ladders.'

'Nip in and get it, Kit, before he comes back.'

Kit did not hesitate. He scrambled towards the cavil, collected the pick, and bundled Dick back through the barricade. As they hurried back they heard the two men behind them calling to each other along the gallery; then the voices grew fainter and fainter till they were inaudible.

The return journey seemed comparatively short, although the boys were troubled by a strange sensation that the earth around them was alive and moving, as if it were breathing and writhing and flexing itself; and they remembered how their father had often told them of the way in which the rocks underground would seem to move in an almost human way, crushing and closing some workings, and opening new paths and passages where none had existed. They squeezed hurriedly through narrow openings where the walls seemed to be closing in on them like

jaws, and at last found themselves once more at the foot
of the staple.

By this time the short candle lengths were down again.
They put in their last pair, and Kit set to work making
handholds in the walls with his pick. About eleven feet up
he dug out a hollow a foot long and about four inches
deep. Then clinging to the wall with feet and one hand,
he drew up the sound section of the ladder, manoeuvred
it with great difficulty through the trapdoor opening, and
wedged the foot in the hole that he had dug. Then very
slowly he edged along the ladder and gained the wooden
platform. A few minutes later Dick had joined him and
they were safe.

Too dirty to dare to go straight home, they took off
their boots and stockings and lit a fire. They cleaned their
boots with twigs, and water from the beck, then washed
their stockings and dried them by the fire. They rubbed

the dirt from their clothes as best they could, washed their hands and faces, and waited for the darkness to come down before they went home.

'Goodness gracious, you both look like a pair of chimney sweeps,' said Hetty when she saw them. 'On the fells? You both look to me as if you've been down the pit.'

But she did not know how correct she was.

No one got to know of the escapade, but it had one strange consequence. A few days later Dick was sitting with his father and mother in the kitchen at home. Kit, who could never sit quietly at home for long, was out somewhere. Mr Ullathorne was sitting in a rocking-chair in front of the fire, reaching out every now and then to run the poker along the bars of the grate, or to break up the coal. He could not stand a dull fire. He liked to crack the black crust open and watch the flames licking up through the coal. His wife was sitting in a basket chair that creaked not only when she moved in it, but of its own accord long after she had got out of it. Dick was sitting on a cracket, counting marbles and dropping them into a blue cloth bag. He was listening to his father and mother as they talked.

'They're having some fun with old Jossie Milburn, by all accounts,' said Mr Ullathorne.

'What's the matter with him?'

'They canna get him to go back to his work – leastways not to his old cavil. Neither God nor the Devil, he says, will get him to go back there.'

'Why not?'

'He says the place is haunted.'

'Haunted?'

'Aye. Seemingly he put his pick down the other day

68

and went to see the deputy, and when he came back it was gone.'

In alarm, Dick dropped a handful of marbles into his bag.

'Dicky, for heaven's sake,' said his mother, 'stop making such a row with them marbles. I cannot hear what your father's saying. What did you say, Davy? He lost his pick?'

'It just vanished. Nobody can account for it. It just disappeared – or at least that's what Jossie says.'

In his agitation Dicky dropped a marble on the floor. His heart came into his mouth, but he put his foot on the marble to stop it from rolling, and waited for his father to go on.

'But surely, Davy,' said Hetty, 'he's not the only one to lose a pick, is he?'

'No. He isn't the first and he won't be the last, but the funny thing is that he was working all by himself. He has a cavil right at the far end of the Busty, and there isn't a man within fifty yards of him.'

'Have they all looked for his pick?'

'Every man jack of them. But nobody can lay eyes on it.'

'Jossie must have been drunk.'

'Drunk? Why, woman, Jossie Milburn's the biggest teetotaller in the colliery. If you ask me what it is, I'd say it was Hob of the Goaf, that's what I'd say it was.'

'What's that, Da?' asked Dick, with his foot still on the marble.

'Some pits have their spirits, Dick. You cannot deny it. Old Tom Danby used to swear by Hob of the Goaf. There's one in every pit – that's what he used to say, and, by sangs, I'm beginning to think he was right.'

'It's very likely, very likely,' replied Hetty. 'But what's

going to happen to Jossie?'

'Well, as luck would have it, the deputy says that the place is nearly worked out anyway. They've been thinking of giving it up for a few months now. It's an awkward cavil. It's right out of the way, and it isn't good coal.'

'So Jossie will get a new cavil?'

'Aye. They'll give him something a bit handier.'

'Will they ever go back to the old place, Da?'

'I don't suppose they will. If it's finished, they'll let the top down and close her in. But, here, I forgot to tell you. When they were looking round for the pick, what do you think they found but a piece of chalk, and Jossie swears he's never used a piece of chalk in all his days as a pitman. Now what the devil would a ghost want with a piece of chalk, eh? . . . Here, Dick, where are you off to?'

Dick, who could stand the suspense no longer, was quietly unlatching the door.

'I'm just going to see our Kit.'

'What for?'

'I have to tell him something – from the teacher.'

'Any excuse to get out, particularly when it's getting on for bedtime. It's a pound to a pinch of salt,' said Hetty, 'that he hasn't a word to say to him.'

She was wrong for the second time. Dick had a great deal to tell his brother, and both of them went in fear and trembling of being found out for many a day. But at last the affair of the lost pick was forgotten, the story of the ghost that haunted the pit ceased to be news, and they breathed again.

8

Growing Up

Slowly the long northern winter settled over the colliery. The winds veered to the north and east, and began to sweep cuttingly down the length of the bleak and open streets. The hawkers' carts churned up the mud that lay between the rows until the women had to lay down paths of ashes to get to the privies. Day after day cloud and smoke blotted out the sun, and the landscape took on a gaunt and bony look.

The women pulled their shawls over their heads and complained about the weather. The men, disdaining overcoats and gloves, thrust their hands deeper into their pockets and tied scarves round their necks. The children played on. They squatted around their home-made braziers and roasted potatoes. They hung around while a pig was being killed, begged the bladder for a football, and kicked it up and down till it burst. At night they burnt paper in the spouts until the flames roared up them and old women flung open their doors in fright. They scudded in and out of the street-lamps, playing tally-ho, knocky-nine-door, barley biscuits, kick-the-block and a score of other games; and if the weather was wet, they sat indoors playing dominoes, and endless card games with greasy old packs.

All these activities contented most of them – but not

Kit. He lay low for a few weeks after the episode of the staple, but neither bad weather nor the fear of discovery could keep him for long out of mischief. Early in the new year temptation appeared in the shape of a rabbit-skin merchant who wanted company. Once more Kit's desk was empty. Once more a growing row of black rings began to appear against his name in the school register. Once more Dick slept alone in the attic.

When at last he came home the scene that had followed his return from Towin Law was repeated. His father stormed at him, threatened him, and forgave him. Although, however, his father's patience was not yet exhausted, there were others who were not prepared to put up with him any more. When he answered his name in class the next morning his teacher paused, looked up, wrote a note and sent it to the Headmaster. A few minutes later an answer came. The great partitions between the classrooms began to slide back, and the whole school was ordered to assemble. It was obvious that something unusual was about to happen. The teachers, instead of standing by their classes, as they usually did, were formed up on either side of Mr Allcroft's desk. He himself looked more like a judge than a headmaster. His face was set in strong horizontal lines, as if his eyebrows, eyes and mouth had all been drawn with a ruler, and the roll of fat on his shoulders seemed heavier than ever. As the last class took up its position a great silence came over the school, a silence so deep that the distant outside noises, usually unnoticed, became audible once more – the muted collision of trucks in the sidings, a far-off buzzer, a clang-clang from the blacksmith's shops. Mr Allcroft allowed the silence to last for a while. Then he called out in a quiet but severe voice:

'Christopher Ullathorne, is he here?'

Kit raised his hand.

'Come to my desk!'

Kit sidled out of his small desk, and walked forward, his big boots resounding on the wooden floor. He showed no sign of alarm. To Dick he looked as fearless as he had done when they had found themselves alone at the bottom of the staple; and if any heart was racing, it was Dick's not Kit's.

'Put out your hand. Your right hand.'

Kit paused for a second, and then lifted his hand and held it palm upwards. Without one word of explanation, Mr Allcroft lifted the cane and brought it down six times.

'Now the left hand.'

Kit paused again for a second as if he was going to refuse, but at last he held it out, and the Headmaster gave him six more cuts. Mr Allcroft was an expert caner. He knew just where to hit, and how to pause just long enough for the pain to subside, but not completely, before striking again. Long experience had taught him how to hurt without doing damage, and the whole school seemed to wince as the cane cut through the air and met the palm. Kit was hurt. Red weals began to appear on his hands, and his face flushed. When the caning was over he tucked his hands in his armpits and hugged them. For a second his head went down. Then it was raised again, and he looked straight at Mr Allcroft, not in hatred nor in repentance, but with a blank look on his face, as if he was determined to reveal no hint of his feelings. It was this that told the Headmaster that he had not really intimidated the boy, and it was this realization, more then anything else, that angered him.

'Turn round!' he cried. 'Face that door! Get out! Keep going till you get out of that door, and never come back!'

Kit turned round and made for his desk. 'Where do you think you're . . .' began Mr Allcroft, but he did not finish. All the school watched Kit. He looked an awkward figure. His knickerbockers were too tight for him, and there was a big brown darn in his grey stocking. The vent in the back of his jacket was split, and the lining was showing through, and the tough hair on the back of his crown stuck up like a brush. He blew once on his hands, then picked up his cap from under his desk, and made for the door. He seemed to be turning something over in his mind, but he made no attempt to retaliate. As he went through the big school door he tried to close it after him, but a piece of coke had been dropped on the floor, and was in the way. He stooped and picked it up. For a moment everyone thought he was going to throw it. Instead he walked back into the classroom, put the piece of coke in the bucket by the fire, turned round and went out, closing the door quietly behind him.

He never went back. That was the end of his schooldays. The next day he was taken on at the colliery.

During the weeks that followed an important change took place in Dick's life, too. The peppery old Mr

Roderick, who had been their teacher for a long time, re-
tired, and his place was taken by a younger man with
curly brown hair, a large ring on his finger, and thin
brown shoes that squeaked as he walked. To Dick he
seemed a creature from another world. He had a soft
southern voice, and he always carried two handkerchiefs,
one to use and one neatly folded in his breast pocket. To
possess enough clean hankies to be able to use two at once
was to Dick an indication of unbelievable wealth; but even
more impressive was the fact that this young man never
seemed to have to raise his voice, or use a cane, or send
boys off to the Headmaster. After the cruelty and enmity
of Mr Roderick, Mr Bradwell seemed a friend. He could
enliven his lessons with quick drawings on the blackboard,
he could make stories seem exciting, but, best of all as far
as Dick was concerned, he could play the piano and sing,
and when the boy heard him at play-time and at dinner-
time playing the school piano and singing –

> I'll sing thee songs of Araby,
> And tales of wild Cashmere . . .

he felt himself immediately transported into another
world.

Dick would often stay behind at school after lessons and
wait for his young teacher to come out. Mr Bradwell lived
at Durham, and had to walk to Branton and back every
day. There was no other form of transport except the railway, and the station was far away on the other side of the
colliery. On fine evenings Dick would wait for him at the
school gate.

'Can I walk home with you, sir?'

'Yes, but you mustn't come too far.'

'Can I carry your case for you, sir?'

'Thank you very much. That's very good of you.'

The road led along the school wall, and then through the allotments, making a narrow lane between the queer poverty-stricken fences that separated plot from plot. In rainy weather a little stream of water ran along this lane, swinging from side to side, and anyone who used it had to zig-zag to dodge the mud. After that the path widened and ran along the side of the Fiery Heap, and as they picked their way across the ashes and the rubbish they would talk.

'I learnt that poem you read to us, sir.'

'Which one was that?'

'"O to be in England", sir.'

'Ah, yes, it's a good poem.'

Dick started on it, and went right through it without faltering.

'Well, you seem to have learnt it very thoroughly. Did you learn it all on your own?'

'Yes, sir, I learnt it at play-time.'

'That's very good, but I think you ought to be turning back now.'

'Just a bit farther, sir.'

'All right, then, just to the stile.'

And when they reached the stile, delighted with having been granted the privilege of carrying Mr Bradwell's case, and of appearing before the world as his friend, Dick turned and ran back to his world of clarty streets and ash-closets.

It was Mr Bradwell who first gave Dick a desire to read, but books were in very short supply in Branton. Many of the miners possessed a Bible and a hymn book, but few owned more than that. Mr Ullathorne, who was not a chapel-goer, did not possess a single volume. There was a collection of dusty technical books in a cupboard at the Institute, but they were not easy to get at, nor were they the kind of books he wanted. Mr Bradwell was willing to lend, but he had few volumes and many pupils. There was indeed only one person in Dick's immediate circle who could help him, and that was his own grandmother.

Old Mrs Ullathorne lived in a little row of houses that stood on the fringe of the colliery. It was a position she liked, for she was an uncommunicative and self-sufficient woman with very little sympathy for the rest of the people in the colliery. She was a tradesman's daughter, and, on the death of her father many years ago, had, for some reason which she never divulged, come north with her mother. They had been robbed on the boat coming from London to Newcastle, and within a few months of landing, her mother had died. Poor, friendless, and hardly knowing where to turn for help, she had married a young pitman and had come to live at Branton; but she had never meant to be a miner's wife, and refused to consider herself as one. She made no friends. She lived almost in seclusion, having set herself the task of working her family back to the position from which she had fallen. She lived frugally, saving everything she could. She had come in the end to have the reputation of being a wealthy woman, but no one knew how much she possessed, and certainly no one dared to ask.

She was very small, and a little hunched, but without one grey hair. She always kept her hair combed backwards, and treated it regularly with a little olive oil to keep it dark and shiny. She wore a black blouse with long sleeves, and a long, full black skirt that swept the ground. Her house was dark and shadowy and no doors were ever left open. Most of the colliery folk had free and easy manners, and were in the habit of popping in and out of one another's houses without knocking; but no one ever dared enter old Mrs Ullathorne's house without permission. The doors of her cupboards and great mahogany press were also kept locked, and the stair door and the pantry door were never left ajar. She had a great dislike of artificial light, and, perhaps out of a habit of economy, would put off lighting the lamps till the very last minute. She would sit by the darkening window polishing her sharp little knives with emery-paper until the light completely failed her. She never spoke like a colliery woman, and never used a dialect word.

To Dick she was a mysterious but attractive figure. He had not been in the habit of visiting her frequently, but now that new worlds were beginning to open up for him he began to turn towards her and her house, where the mat-frames never cluttered the floor, and no talkative neighbours ever came. After the racket of the streets he liked to retire there, where only the ticking of the clock disturbed the silence.

In size and arrangement his grandmother's kitchen was like hundreds of others in Branton. There was a table, pushed up against the window and covered in oil-cloth, a press, a sewing machine, a horsehair sofa, a large black range with an oven on one side and a copper on the other side of the grate, and a rocking-chair. In the alcove under the stairs, however, there was a bed with iron bed-ends decorated with brass knobs, and at the foot of the bed, on a little shelf tucked away under the stairs, a small row of books. It was a strange collection – *The Pilgrim's Progress*, an old almanac, a *Tour of Rome, Oliver Twist*, and *The Holly Tree Inn*, two or three old school readers, and a book on the diseases of horses.

Dick was never allowed to take these books as he wished. He had always first to ask permission and to wash his hands. Then he had to promise not to make any marks on the pages. When he had satisfied these requirements he could choose and begin to read.

He could make little of the *Tour of Rome*, and was not ready for the Bunyan and *The Holly Tree Inn*; but he liked to terrify himself by looking again and again at the illustrations to *Oliver Twist*, particularly the picture of Fagin in the condemned cell, with the grim noose visible through the bars. He would secretly trace the outlines of the noble stallions and mares in the horse book; and strangely enough he was fond of the old school readers

79

with their story poems and moral tales. Many of these little stories ended with a short vocabulary list –

altitude – height
profundity – depth

He was greatly attracted by these words. He wrote them down and memorized them, and planned to use them the next time Mr Bradwell gave the class a composition. 'The lake was of great profundity. The altitude of the mountain was immense.' He imagined Mr Bradwell lifting his eyebrows as he came to such magnificent words. What a lovely sound they had . . . 'altitude', 'profundity'.

He got so much pleasure out of his reading that he fell into the habit of staying late, hoping that he might be allowed to stay the night, but it was only on very rare occasions that he was allowed that privilege. Generally he was dismissed after supper which always consisted of bread and hard American cheese. On those late evenings when he ran home through the darkness and the silence the colliery seemed to be a different place, more secret, more furtive, more mysterious.

In the meanwhile, Kit had settled to his new life as a pitman. Mr Ullathorne, who had more of his mother in him than he thought, had been a little disappointed at having to put his son into the mine before he had meant to, but for Kit himself it was a good move. He had been ready for work for a long time, and he took to the mine like a duck to water. Before long he was promoted to pony-putting, that is, hauling with the help of a pony the full tubs from the coal-face to the bottom of the shaft; and he gloried in the work. He had hated school, but in the pit he was at home, and all his old restlessness and discontent began to leave him.

Now that they were pitmen together the bond between Kit and his father began to strengthen, and Dick was drawn more and more towards his school work and his grandmother. The old woman, disappointed in her pitman son, began to hope that her grandson would help her to fulfil some of her secret ambitions. She rarely gave him money, but she encouraged him to read, and to talk to her about school. 'Your father was a good scholar,' she said, 'but he was bent on working in the pit. But you'll be something yet before you're finished.'

Once when he called he found a stranger with her, a neatly dressed old man with a sharp little beard, spats, and a carnation in his button-hole. It was her brother, who owned a saw-mill in the south, and who had come to visit her. Dick did not know that he had such wealthy and important relations, and the realization that not all his people were pitmen gave him a strange surprise.

'This is David's boy, George. His youngest,' said his grandmother.

The old man bent towards him, and Dick could see the dark centre of his flower, and smell the cigar on his breath.

'How old is he?'

'How old are you now, Richard?'

'I'm nearly twelve.'

'He's small, but what a wonderful pair of eyes he has, Elizabeth. I'd give a hundred pounds for a pair of eyes like that.'

It gave Dick a pleasant feeling to hear that his eyes were worth so much. He had not been used to thinking of any part of himself as worth anything. When his grandmother said, 'Yes, George, we'll see him something yet,' he began for the first time to believe her.

Only a short time after Kit had left school, however, an event happened which threatened to put the old woman's hopes beyond the reach of fulfilment.

9

The Strike

One day when Dick was hanging about the pithead waiting for his brother to come up, he saw someone drive up
to the office in a trap. Although he had seen them in the
dark only, he recognized the pony and the trap at once;
and although the man who got out bore little resemblance
to the sick, hunched figure he had helped to get home, he
recognized him too. It was Mr Sleath the owner of the
colliery; and Dick felt an impulse to run up to him and
ask if he remembered the boy who had found him nearly
dead in the ditch near Broomilaw.

Dick watched him go into the office and then come out
with Mr Curtiss the colliery manager. Mr Sleath was the
smaller of the two, with a cleanshaven but dark face with
two strong lines sloping across his cheeks like the sides of
a triangle. He carried a stick but there was something in
his walk that made him look like a miner in spite of his
good clothes. Dick hid himself behind the wall of one of
the repair shops as they came past him and went to the
top of the shaft. They stood there watching the coal come
to the surface.

The coal came up in the same cages as those used for the
men. It was sent up in heavy squat tubs that packed tightly
into the cages. As each cage reached the top the doors were
flung open and the tubs were trundled out towards the big

moving belts on which the coal was sorted. There were
boys and old men on each side of these belts, and it was
their job to sort the good coal from the useless stone that
sometimes got into the tubs. If a tub contained too much
stone the man who had filled it got nothing at all for it.
This was a system that the men hated, but Mr Sleath
would not alter it.

By now they had got on to the platform that stood between the belts and the top of the shaft, and a gentle wind
carried all that they said to Dick's ears in spite of the noise
of the machinery.

'Mr Curtiss,' Mr Sleath said, poking forward with his

stick, 'these tubs are not full.'

He indicated with his stick the tubs that were being trundled by him to the belts. They were not full to the brim; the coal had been loosely heaped in them.

'They're as full as they can be, Mr Sleath,' replied the manager. 'All these come out of the Ballarat. There's only a few inches there between the tub and the roof. It's bad enough filling them as it is.'

'But they aren't full. I pay for full tubs, not for half-empty ones. This is robbery. I am being systematically cheated.'

'I don't see how we can remedy the situation, Mr Sleath, conditions being what they are.'

'Don't you? Well, I do.'

'We'll always have to make an exception of that particular seam, Mr Sleath.'

'Nonsense. I'll show you a way. Fetch me two big fellows from the belts.'

Two of the bigger boys were brought over, and Mr Sleath gave them their instructions.

'Now you two get hold of that tub and rock it.'

'Which way?'

'There's only one way of rocking it – like a cradle. Rock it from side to side and shake down that coal.'

The tub was not easy to rock, but the boys eventually did it, and to Mr Sleath's undisguised satisfaction the coal settled at a level well below the level of the sides of the tub.

'There you are! What did I tell you? These men have been cheating me for years. Every tub that's come out of the pit must have been nearly a quarter empty. Now take down these instructions, Mr Curtiss: all full tubs in all seams are from today onwards to be rocked at the coal-face until the coal in the tub settles at a level, and this level must be not more than one inch below the level of the sides of the tub. Have you got that? Good.'

As he turned away he caught sight of Dick, who was standing by a truck, and appearing to take a keen interest in the proceedings.

'What's this boy doing here?'

'I suppose he's waiting for the shift to end, Mr Sleath.'

'Come here, boy. Do you work here?'

'No.' In his confusion Dick forgot his manners.

'Then what are you doing here? Don't you know that you're not supposed to be here? How does it come about, Mr Curtiss, that you allow these ragamuffins to run about on my premises? What's your name, boy?'

'Richard Ullathorne.'

'Does your father work here?'

'Yes, sir. He works in the Ballarat.'

'Does he, now? Well, just you cut and run, otherwise both you and your father will be getting into trouble. See that?'

'Yes, sir.'

'And see this?' Mr Sleath lifted up his stick. 'Well, get away from this yard before I lay it across your back. It beats me, Mr Curtiss, how you cannot keep normal pit discipline in your yard. Have you got that notice?'

'Yes, Mr Sleath.'

'Right. I want no more half-empty tubs, and I expect you to see to it that I don't get any.'

He walked away without saying good morning, and Dick, who had retreated beyond the blacksmith's shop, turned to look at him. He could hardly believe that this was the man whom he had helped and who had given him

86

a two-shilling piece. Now he could understand why his father hated him. As the trap rolled away, he bent down and picked up a stone.

It would have given him great pleasure to have hit those detested shoulders or at least to spoil the paintwork on that trap. Fortunately, he thought better of it. He kept the stone till he came to the pond, threw it in the middle of the water, and ran off home.

Two days later the instruction given by Mr Sleath was issued. For three days after that the men tried to observe it, and then they began to mutiny.

When at the end of the third day Dick's father came home from the pit, the boy could hardly recognize him. His face, usually happy and mischievous, was dark and angry. His eyes seemed unusually white and restless, and even beneath his pit dirt you could see that his jaw was set and his mouth shut tight.

'Get that lad off to bed, Hetty,' he shouted, as soon as he came in. 'It's time he was upstairs.'

'Why, Davy, it's not what you'd call late. Surely he can stay up till you get bathed.'

'I'll have my supper first.'

'What, before you get washed?'

'Aye.'

'There must be something up for you to have your supper before you get washed.'

'Never mind about that. Get him off to bed.'

'But, Da, it's only . . .'

'No back-answering! Upstairs, do you hear?'

Dick looked in bewilderment at his father. He had never seen him so bad-tempered. He was not a man who lost his temper easily, but now he seemed irritated and touchy, and there was a new note in his voice. Dick went upstairs, but he was so curious that he left the attic door ajar.

He could make out very little. At first he could hear his mother speaking very quietly, trying to soothe her husband and to get him to eat; but David was not so easily calmed. He began to raise his voice, and odd angry phrases reached the attic . . . 'More than flesh and blood can stand . . .' 'What does he think we are, lackeys?' . . . 'I tell you, Hetty, if we let him get away with this, he'll trample on us' . . . 'But he'll get something he hasn't bargained for . . .' Dick could hear his mother protesting, but in the end it sounded as if she had given in to him. There was a long conversation, subdued and earnest. Then Dick heard the backdoor open and his father go across the yard.

When his father was beyond the gate Dick got out of bed and opened the skylight. He could see that his father was still in his pit clothes and had not even washed his face. He was hurrying to the other side of the street where about thirty or forty men had collected under the feeble street-lamp. They were all talking excitedly, passing papers that looked like pay-notes from one to the other, and holding them up to examine them in the faint light. As they talked, more and more men joined them, and a few women appeared at the gates, their white pinafores glimmering in the darkness. Dick heard the men shouting at two inquisitive boys who were hanging around on the edge of the group. Then a silence came over the gathering, and they all seemed to be looking inward and paying attention to someone in the centre of the circle who was putting forward some kind of proposal. When he had finished there was a moment of hesitation, and then the crowd began to disperse. All up and down the street Dick could hear doors and gates being opened and closed, and although it was late there was a light burning in every kitchen. For a long time Mr and Mrs Ullathorne sat talking. Then at last Dick heard the hot water being poured into the zinc bath, and he fell asleep.

The next day the whole colliery was humming with excitement. The men had called a mass meeting and had decided to come out on strike against the infamous rocking-rule that Mr Sleath had imposed upon them.

The strike began immediately, and an uncanny silence fell upon the colliery. The nights were undisturbed by the caller, no tankies fussed and laboured up the line to the fells, no buzzers blew, no hammering came from the shops, no sounds of shunting from the sidings. Except when the safetymen went down to keep an eye on the pumps and to inspect the idle machinery, the pulleys were still, and the big condenser ceased to steam and fume. During the first few days two or three blacklegs tried to stay at work, but the pickets waited for them as they came up, and gave them a rough handling. By the end of the week they too had joined the strikers and the stoppage was complete.

By that time Mr Sleath had made up his mind how to answer the challenge. He had been advised not to show himself in the colliery, and he was prudent enough to respect the advice. But he knew how to act, and in the solitude of his great ugly house he prepared his plans.

10

The Candymen

For the first few days of the strike the men were content to take a holiday. Many spent their time in the Institute, playing endless games of billiards and making up card schools, or drinking in the gaunt blackened public house that stood just outside the colliery yard; but the more prudent and thoughtful avoided gambling and beer. They took to walking in the lanes and across the fields, although with their pale faces and awkward gait they were hardly at home there. They leant over gates, looking at hedges and crops and animals, or sat on their 'unkers' behind stone walls, staring at the wide landscape, and talking. But they were not used to idling, and after a few days they began to look around for something to put their hands to. The women, too, who were not used to having the men in the house all day, began to grow a little restless.

Fortunately the weather began to clear, and it was mild enough to work outside. Kit had by this time a dozen pigeons, and his father helped him to repair and enlarge the pigeon cree that stood in the waste weedy garden behind the house. All day long they were busy hammering and sawing, nailing down odd pieces of roofing felt, and painting black and white vertical stripes on the front of the cree. Kit had more time to train the birds, and he took them regularly on to the fells and released them there.

Dick would hurry home from school to watch the birds flying in, and to wheedle them down on to the traps, calling 'Bucketacoo, bucketacoo...' and throwing grains of Indian corn to them.

A few weeks after the beginning of the stoppage the miners began to run short of household coal. When they were at work, of course, they were allowed a certain amount of coal as part of their wages, but now that they were on strike the allowance had ceased. As supplies in the coal-houses began to dwindle, the men turned, as they always did, to the Fiery Heap. In certain parts of the heap it was possible to sieve the slag and recover the small pieces of coal and coke that had been discarded with it.

It was a slow business winning this coal, and a great deal of slag had to be worked over before one bag of worthwhile fuel could be collected; but it was congenial work. It gave the men the feeling that they were back at work, and, what was more important, it kept their muscles and their hands in good trim. As soon as a pitman ceased to work his hands grew soft, and when he returned to his pick and shovel they blistered and bled. All the men disliked too the great stiffness that came upon them when they resumed work after being laid off for some time. They were happy to work on the heap, because it kept them fit, as well as filling the empty coal-houses.

Dick resented having to go to school on these days.

Even though he was still fond of Mr Bradwell, he would rather have been working on the cree, or taking the pigeons up to the fells, or digging on the Fiery Heap; but the evenings brought him some compensation. His father very rarely went out after dark. There was no money now for a drink or a game of cards at the club. He stayed in and busied himself with indoor jobs such as cobbling, and Dick would work with him, handing him the sprigs or the hammer, and melting the heelball for him. Sometimes, when there was nothing urgent to do, they would get out the cards and all four sit round the table in the hot kitchen playing whist or rummy.

These were unexpectedly happy days. So far the strike had brought little hardship or suffering. Strike pay was not high, but it continued to come in. Savings had not yet been exhausted. Pantries were still reasonably full, and clothes reasonably sound. At the beginning of the fourth week, however, when all attempts to come to an agreement had come to nothing, a change came over the scene. In the solitude of Sion House Mr Sleath had prepared his master plan. He now proceeded to put it into practice.

Branton possessed a railway station, a mean, draughty structure with two short platforms, one dingy waiting-room and a smoke-blackened bridge. The railway was generally far busier hauling coal than men or women, and few passengers used the station. On the Tuesday of the fourth week of the strike, however, the morning train unloaded at Branton no less than fifty passengers.

They were not miners. Their faces, their clothes, and their gait all made that clear. They were rough-looking in another way, with red eyes, pasty and blotched faces, and crumpled clothes. Dirty flannel shirts showed above greasy

94

waistcoats, and around their necks were knotted soiled scarves. They were the dreaded 'candymen', the riff-raff of the Newcastle and Sunderland wharf and dockside doss-houses, loungers, loafers and thugs enlisted by Mr Sleath to carry out the punishment which he had planned.

There were ten policemen to meet them. Among them, and looking ill at ease, was Branton's own constable; and these policemen, after putting the men in rough order, began to march them towards the colliery. It was a ragged march. The candymen had not only been given a hearty breakfast, they had also been freely plied with liquor; but the liquor had not so much fuddled them as made them insolent. They swaggered on, and the knowledge that authority and the law were, for once, on their side, went to their heads.

As they drew nearer to the heart of the colliery, doors were flung open and windows lowered, and women in aprons and men in shirt sleeves appeared in doorways and at the top of steps to look at them. They all had the surprised look of a people who had suddenly been invaded and unexpectedly conquered, and whose country was to be occupied. Only children and dogs ran out to have a closer look, and to follow the gang as it moved past Sinker's Row, across the open patch by the fish shop and the Methodist Chapel, past the coal depots and on to Chapel Row.

The first house in the row, the house nearest the depots, was occupied by a childless couple, Elijah and Sarah Ann Lee. They were meek people, good-living and devout chapel-goers. Elijah was a local preacher, and his wife, with no children to care for, loved her house. She always had the doors and windows painted at her own expense, and put old stocking-legs on the legs of her tables and chairs to keep them from being scratched. She kept her top step carefully whitened, and even – a feat almost unheard-of in Branton – had got a laurel-bush to take root in a hole in the corner of the yard.

It was before her house that the candymen stopped.

'Are you Elijah Lee?' asked the policeman who was in charge.

'I am,' said Elijah. He had come to the door in his shirt sleeves and stockinged feet. He had been reading his daily chapter of Scripture and was still wearing his spectacles.

'Are you on strike?'

'I am.'

'And are you prepared to go back to work tomorrow?'

'On whose terms, mister?'

'On Mr Sleath's.'

'Never in all this world. If Mr Sleath has come to an agreement with us, I'll go back to work and give thanks to God. But not a minute before!'

'Right. We have orders to evict you, and a lot like you. Get your clothes on and get outside. We don't want no trouble. Come on, you fellows, get started.'

'But you can't turn us out of house and home!'

'Make him show his warrant, 'Lijah!' cried one of the neighbours. News about the eviction had spread quickly, and a crowd had already collected.

'Ye needn't worry, Jack,' replied one of the candymen. 'We have warrants for the lot of you.'

He walked straight into the house before it could be locked against him, and called out to his mates to begin, and before Elijah could recover his wits the overseer of the candymen had pulled the key out of the lock, and the eviction had begun.

Everything in the tidy house was brought out and dumped either in the yard or in the street; and at the same time other teams were at work clearing the second, third, fourth, fifth and sixth houses.

Of all this Dick saw nothing. The schoolchildren were kept in ignorance of what was happening, and at dinner-time when Dick came out of school he was met by Kit, who told him he had to go and have dinner with his grand-mother.

All through afternoon-school rumours were flying, but Dick could not properly understand them; and when he went home for tea, he could scarce believe what he saw. Every house in Chapel Row had been cleared, every family had been evicted, and the street looked as if some great sale was in preparation.

All the yards were stacked with beds, tables, wardrobes, mirrors, presses and wash-hand stands, while the com-moner articles of furniture, stools, chairs, forms and mangles, all stood with their legs sunk into the street mud. The women wept to see their treasured furniture standing unprotected against the damp winter evening, their bed-clothes and table-cloths dragging in the dirt, and all that they had slaved to keep clean and folded, now thrown carelessly into baskets and drawers. The shame of being without a home, of seeing all their secret possessions dragged out into the common air, of having all that they prized treated like worthless rubbish – all this had been too much for them. They covered their faces with their aprons and wept.

The situation, however, was not hopeless. The people of the colliery were used to helping one another. All doors opened to the evicted families, and all the evening men and boys went backwards and forwards carrying the furniture indoors. Big fires were lit in the streets, and all the helpers worked like coolies until everything was once more under cover. Then when the work was finished the men came out and sat round the street fires, and talked of their next move.

Mrs Ullathorne and her husband were taken in by one of her sisters who lived in Russell Street, Kit found shelter with one of his fellow-putters, and Dick was allowed to stay with his grandmother. For him the disaster was more like a holiday, for the old woman spoiled him, let him sleep in the alcove where the books were, and gave him a duck egg for breakfast.

The candymen had made it plain that their task was only half-finished, and everyone in the colliery knew that they would be back the next day.

'There'll be ructions here tomorrow,' said Mr Ullathorne to Dick, 'and you'd better keep yourself out of the way, lad, if you don't want to get hurt. Stop with your grandmother, that's a good lad.'

His warning, far from scaring Dick, made him only the keener to see the candymen for himself. He didn't go to school at all that morning, but followed a gang of boys who had heard that the men were preparing to give the candymen a rough welcome. They found the men collected on the station bridge, and lining the path that ran along the embankment above the waiting-room. Dick saw his father there, and hung back.

The candymen arrived as before, but this time, as soon as they got out of the train, they were greeted with a shower of stones and mud. Dick was not slow to join in the attack, and he didn't know whether to be delighted or terrified when his stone bounded off the roof of the waiting-room and hit one of the thugs between the shoulders. The constables, however, had made their preparations, too. They were all armed, and while the candymen took refuge in the waiting-room, the officer-in-charge stepped forward and called up to the men who were swarming on the railings at the top of the embankment.

'Now cut that out up there! I've got orders to protect these men and if any of you hinders them in the execution of their duty, you'll find yourselves in clink. And if there's any monkey business I may as well tell you that I'm empowered to read the Riot Act, and God help the men who hang around once I've done that. Now, come on, make up your minds to behave yourselves. Use your common savvy, and let's have no more trouble.'

The men did not move, but they were momentarily cowed, and threw no more stones. The policemen got their men out of the waiting-room, lined them up and led them off once more in the direction of the colliery. Baffled and despairing, the strikers followed them this time to Russell Street, and there the shameful scenes of the previous day were repeated. By the end of the short winter day one more street of houses had been cleared and locked and the keys taken away; and once more the darkness fell on piles of unprotected furniture and on homeless families.

The candymen, however, did not escape entirely scot-free. When they were retreating past Sinker's Row, with Dick and the other boys dogging their heels and waiting for an opportunity to have a go at them, one of the women, who was standing at her door with a blazer in her hand and a black-leading brush in the other, suddenly brandished them both, and began to beat the brush against the blazer. It was a wounderful sound. To Dick it was like a drum calling to battle. When the beating was taken up by more women, and he saw them rushing out like Amazons, it was an invitation he could not resist.

'Charge!' he shouted.

There was no need to look for weapons. Every boy was already armed with a stone. Women and boys rushed forward and a volley fell on the backs of the retreating candymen. By now all their dutch courage had forsaken them. Like the cowards they were they broke ranks and ran, and did not stop till they reached the safety of the station. It was a bruised and spattered crew that climbed aboard the Newcastle train that night; and though Dick and the rest of the truants were well and truly caned the next morning, it was a very small price to pay for such a glorious victory.

Mr Sleath was not slow to retaliate. The next day a notice was pinned on the door of the colliery offices saying that every householder who dared to take in any member of an evicted family would also be turned out. Then everyone realized that the strike had become a bitter struggle, and the whole colliery prepared for the worst.

That night the men met once more, and Mr Ullathorne was deputed to speak for those who had been evicted. Not one of them, he said, wanted to give in. This last action of Mr Sleath's had made them all the more determined to fight on. No one, however, wanted to be the cause of more evictions. They were very grateful to all their friends who had taken them in, but they knew that if they went on accepting their hospitality the whole colliery would be evicted. What he would ask the Union to do would be to provide tents for all the homeless families. The Rushy

Field was common land. Nobody could turn them away from there, and although it was winter-time they were all prepared to put up with cold and discomfort rather than give in.

The next day a deputation was sent to Durham to the Union Headquarters. They came back with the assurance that bell-tents and marquees would be provided; and the strike continued.

11

Under Canvas

The Rushy Field was so-called because along its lower edge, which was damp, there grew a fringe of bullrushes; but the upper slopes were drier, and there was one reasonably flat stretch, sheltered from the north by a line of sycamores, and large enough to take the tents. The fields had always been a favourite playground for the colliery folk. The children used to roll their 'paste eggs' down the slopes at Easter, and on fine summer evenings whole families would sit on the slopes enjoying the view across the roofs of the colliery streets, picking out the landmarks – the distant cathedral, the slag heaps of other collieries, and the foothills of the Pennines climbing gently up to the high fells. Some time ago Mr Sleath had driven a drift into the side of the field, claiming that the mineral rights were his. His claim had been upheld, but he had been disappointed in the yield, and had given up the working. The partly-opened drift was still to be seen, its cavern-like mouth now boarded up, with a thin trickle of reddish water issuing from under the boards. The field was rather open and bleak, but not far away there was a spring of good water, and between it and the colliery lay a group of allotments, many of them with little shacks that the men had made themselves. Many of these were cosy little huts, boasting even stoves and wall-paper; there the men could talk and play cards when the weather was bad.

Most of the tents were too small to take much furniture, but the men purloined as much timber as they could and fitted them out with floors. Bedding, chairs and tables were installed. One marquee was fitted up as a soup-kitchen, and the women washed and mangled and ironed in another. For the boys this was a wonderful adventure, and for Dick it was a dream come true. Overnight he became the backwoodsman, the explorer, the marooned sailor of Mr Bradwell's books, breathing in the wonderful smell of crushed grass under the canvas, collecting timber, lighting fires, digging pits, and exploring the wonders of his new world. He climbed the trees, went in and out of the hedges, prised open the drift-boards and peered into the mysterious darkness of its workings, and at night sat plying the camp-fire with fallen wood and seeing the stars through the smoke and the sparks. It was fortunate for all the strikers that the weather stayed kind and mild. Every morning the women woke up and dreaded the time when the cold east wind would begin to blow across the slope of the hill and through the worn canvas of their shelters; but mercifully the winds slept, and life was not unendurable.

A few days after they had moved into their tents there occurred an incident that put heart into them. Three or four of the women who were still in possession of their homes and kitchens made their way up to the camp, just after breakfast. Each woman carried in her apron a loaf, which she left without a word on the turf outside the larger marquee. The grass was dry, and in the pale winter sunshine the loaves lay and shone like offerings; and when one of the evicted women made as if to collect them, the others restrained her.

'Let them lie there for a bit, Mary Annie. Let folks see that we still have good friends. We may be turned out of house and home, but we still have somebody that thinks about us, thank God!'

So the gift that was offered with dignity was accepted with dignity; and while someone stood by to keep off the dogs and the children, more women appeared from the colliery. The pile of loaves grew. Soon the word ran like wildfire through the streets, and there was scarce a woman still left in her house who did not take a loaf from her bin or her oven to add to the offering. Then when the pile had grown high, Sarah Ann, the wife of the quiet, devout Elijah who had been the first to be evicted, had an inspiration. Picking up the loaves, she began to set them out on the slope behind the tents, first in letters, then in words, until written in golden bread across the hillside read the inspiring sentence –

GOD WILL PROVIDE

At the close of the afternoon when it was growing too late to leave the bread out any longer, Elijah and some of his friends collected round the loaves, and struck up the hymn that they loved –

> Praise God from whom all blessings flow,
> Praise Him all creatures here below,
> Praise Him above, ye heavenly host,
> Praise Father, Son and Holy Ghost.

As the darkness began to fall they lifted up their voices in praise of the goodness that had prompted their neighbours to remember them when the rest of the world seemed to be forgetting them.

Dick stood by watching them. He was puzzled. He still did not properly understand what was happening, and could not make out why, in spite of the gift of bread, so many of the women were crying.

The Secret of Branton Hill

During these weeks Dick became friends with a boy called
Peter Fairless who lived in Cobden Terrace. He was a quiet,
clever boy who was in Dick's class and had been put in
one of the back desks with him. Like most of the Branton
boys he loved to be out in the open air, and Dick and he
would go off as often as they could, 'stravaiging around
the countryside' as Mrs Ullathorne put it.

Just over the rise beyond the tents there was a long lane
lined with sycamore and stunted oaks that led to their
favourite playground. It was a long sloping field of furze
that ended in a rectangular clayey pond with one open
side. Their favourite game was to work their way cautiously up to the top of the field, dodging from clump to
clump as if they were surrounded on all sides by enemies,
and then, having reached the upper end of the field, to go
steeplechasing down, furiously and recklessly, leaping over
every bush that was in their way. It was a law of the game
not to shirk a jump, and when they came to the bottom
their legs were always scratched and prickled. They would
throw themselves down on the banks of the pond until
their wind came back. It was a glorious game. In spite of
the occasional appearance of a gamekeeper or a farmhand
this little field was their kingdom, a territory that no other
boys seemed to want, a land so much their own that they

began to give their names to its features. The little pond was christened Lake Ullathorne, the steeplechase course was the Fairless Ride, and the lane leading to them the Venturers' Way.

They could not wade in the lake. It was too muddy, and the water was too cold; but they sailed logs across it, pulled up the dead shoots of mare's-tail, threw berries at floating leaves, and drove little flotillas of sticks from side to side. Then, when they were tired of these games, they turned to the little pools that had formed all round the pond in the clayey soil after the rain, little lakes of clear rain-water through which you could look at the brown and yellow leaves laid layer on layer on the floor of the pool. The curled and coloured leaves seemed preserved there, as if they had been laid up in isinglass. They plunged their hands into the cold water, touched the berries and acorns lying there, built banks around the pools, gave them all names, but, always under some compulsion which they did not understand, kept the beautiful underwater patterns undisturbed. One day when they were kneeling over one of their little water-museums they both had the feeling that they were being watched; and when they looked up they saw, looking steadily and fearlessly at them, a stoat, its inquisitive head high, its fine white breast clearly visible. For a moment Dick had the strange feeling that it had recognized him. They looked into each other's eyes. Then the stoat turned slowly away and was gone as silently as it had appeared. Day after day they waited for it to come again, but it never reappeared. Dick could not get rid of the feeling that it had known this was their kingdom, and had left it to them.

After these hours of 'stravaiging' in the open air Mrs

Fairless's house seemed wonderfully cosy and homely. Mr Fairless, like Dick's father, had been one of the instigators of the strike, but fortunately he lived in Cobden Terrace and nobody had been evicted from that row. Dick liked to go to Peter's house to play draughts and listen to Mr Fairless's conversation. He was a tall, thoughtful man, with pockets not at the sides but at the front of his trousers, so that when he stood up with his hands thrust into them he looked very straight and very dignified. Dick was fascinated by a way he had of looking straight ahead as if he were gazing at something that no one else could see; and he often watched him with great curiosity as he sat writing letters with a little silver-looking pen with a nib that could slide back into the holder. Mr Ullathorne rarely wrote a letter; in fact they had no ink in the house, and whenever there was a letter to be sent off Dick had to go and borrow a bottle from old Mrs Maddison. But Mr Fairless had his own bookcase, with a glass front, and under it a bureau with small drawers and pigeon-holes.

One night Mr Fairless was sitting playing draughts with the boys when there came a knock at the door, and in answer to the invitation 'Come in!' there entered a visitor that Dick had never seen before. He was a short man with a pointed red beard and sharp ears that seemed to rise to a point. He was well dressed, with a silver watch-chain that went in two loops from pocket to pocket; and Dick noticed that when he held out his hand to Mr Fairless he kept it wide open with the thumb sticking sharply up.

'Well, this is a nice surprise, Mr Candlin,' said Mrs Fairless, getting up and putting down her knitting. 'Can I get you anything to eat?'

'It's a pleasure to come, Mrs Fairless,' replied Mr Candlin, 'and I wish I could enjoy it more frequently. I'll take a cup of tea, if you please. Nobody makes tea like you.'

He spoke in an educated but unaffected voice that was somehow lovely to listen to, and Dick found himself staring at him with great curiosity. He was not used to seeing fine clothes or listening to polished accents.

'It's a sight for sore eyes to see you again, Mark,' said Mr Fairless. 'You carry on with your game, lads, while I talk to Mr Candlin.'

'That's Peter, your boy, I know,' said Mr Candlin, transferring his attention to the table. 'But who's the other young man?'

'This is Dick ... Richard Ullathorne to give him his Sunday name. Come on, Dick, shake hands with the gentleman.'

Dick shook hands with Mr Candlin and felt his soft palm. There were few men in Branton who had hands like this. And again he noticed the hand widely stretched, like the hand of a man who enjoyed meeting people.

'They look a couple of bright young shavers to me. Are you still both at school?'

'Yes, sir.'

'I'm glad to hear it. But don't be in a hurry to leave. Learn all you can, boys, and you'll never be sorry. Well, Flem,' (turning back to Mr Fairless), 'I'm glad to find you in, but I'm sorry to hear that you're all idle again.'

'Yes, we're all men of leisure now.'

'Well, it's an ill wind that blows nobody any good, and this little holiday of yours . . .'

'I'd hardly call it that, Mark.'

'No, you're right; I should have said "this enforced leisure of yours". Whatever it is, it may give us a chance to carry out that little bit of excavation that we've been talking about for so long. You got my letter about it, didn't you?'

'Yes, I've read it very carefully.'

'I don't want anybody to do this job but you, Flem. You're the only one I know that has both the theoretical and the practical knowledge. Do you think you can take it on?'

'I can't deny that I have the time for it.'

'Good. But there's one thing I want to get straight at the outset. I'll engage you only on condition you're paid for it.'

'That's the last thing in my mind.'

'I know, but the labourer is worthy of his hire, and nobody knows that better than you. When do you think you can start?'

'It's a poor time of the year.'

'Yes, but we seem to be in for a mild spell. Can you start this week?'

'I can start tomorrow, if I know where to start.'

'That's fine. Come on, let's have a look at these diagrams I've prepared and I'll show you how I think we ought to tackle it.'

'Clear the table then, lads,' said Mr Fairless. 'Do you mind if they stop, Mark? There's nowhere else I can put them unless they go outside.'

'Not a bit, not a bit. Let them stay and let them listen if they like. These things aren't secrets. The more they hear about them, the better I'm pleased.'

The boys took their game and went on playing on the floor. It seemed bad manners to listen too closely but Dick's curiosity was so great that he gave only half his attention to the draughts board. From time to time strange words caught his ears, words that resembled the fine language he had loved to read in his grandmother's books . . . 'burial chamber' . . . 'funeral trappings' . . . 'possibly cremated' . . . 'careful excavation'. He did not understand them all, and his lack of understanding made him all the more curious to know what mysterious task Mr Fairless was promising to undertake for the stranger.

He was not left in doubt for long. When Mr Candlin had gone Mr Fairless took the boys into his confidence.

'You've just seen a great man, Dicky. Mr Candlin knows more about history and more about what's under the face of this earth than anybody I know. I've been to many of his lectures, and I tell you, lad, it's like music listening to him when he starts talking about history. Ever since I told him about that queer-looking mound on the top of Branton Hill he's been itching to see what's inside it.'

'Which mound, Mr Fairless?'

'Hout, Dick, you'll have seen it dozens of times. It's that bump right on the top of the hill, past the drifts.'

'And is there anything inside that?'

'There may be.'

'I thought it was just a heap of earth. Just sand and stones.'

'And you may be right. But Mr Candlin doesn't think so, and believe me, he's not often wide of the mark. Anyhow, my job is to dig a way into it and find out, and I dare say that will keep me busy for a few days.'

'What do you think you'll find in it, Dad?' asked Peter.

'Maybe a few nice lumps of coal – and they'd come in very handy, too.'

The thought that the common little bump which he had climbed many a time when he had been up on the fells gathering blaeberries might contain something more than just stones and soil, struck Dick so forcibly that as soon as he could he went to have another look at it; but Mr Fairless had already been at work. There was a fence around it, and a tunnel like a drift had been driven into it. There was a door on the entrance, but it was securely locked. He remembered Kit's device for opening locked doors, but even if he had had a screw-driver he would not have used it. He knew that Mr Fairless would tell him as soon as any discovery was made.

Exactly one week after the digging had begun, Mr Fairless did make his discovery. Peter told him about it and he went straight from school to Cobden Terrace.

'What is it, Mr Fairless? Is it treasure?'

'Now don't get excited, Dick. Don't let thy imagination run away with thee. It's nothing but what we thought it would be – a big stone coffin.'

'Is there anything in it?'

'Oh, I haven't opened it yet. That's Mr Candlin's job. I just do the navvying, and it's odds on there'll be nothing but a pile of dust. But there she is – lying just where Mr Candlin said she would, and all we have to do now is to get the top off and hope for the best.'

'Do you think Dick and me could watch Mr Candlin opening it?'

'Not a hope. There's hardly room for two of us inside there, never mind about four. You would just be in the way. Besides you might get the shock of your lives.'

'We wouldn't be frightened.'

'What, not frightened of looking into a coffin? There's

Dick looking a bit sick just at the mention of it.'

'I'm not, Mr Fairless. I'm not frightened of coffins.'

'Nay, I couldn't ask Mr Candlin a thing like that. But he might let you have a look when he's finished.'

Remembering how Mr Candlin had spoken on the evening he had come to Mr Fairless's house, Dick felt that he would not disappoint them; and he was right. He promised that if they found anything that was worth seeing he would let them into the chamber, and to make it possible for them to be there he arranged for the lid to be lifted on a Saturday when they would be free all day.

Early on the appointed day he arrived by train from Durham. Mr Fairless had hired a trap for him and met him at the station. To spare the pony the boys walked up the hill and they all met at the mound. There the pony and trap were handed over to the boys to look after, and the men entered the tunnel, locking the door after them.

The boys had plenty to do to occupy their time. They unharnessed the pony and tethered it where it could graze; and then they kept themselves warm jumping over the low gorse-bushes and running in and out of the heather. They found a small quarry where water had collected in a shallow pool, and floated old pit props across it, pelting them with stones. Then they found a sheltered corner, and got a fire going. There was not much fuel to be found, but they kept it burning with dried heather stalks. The stalks burnt quickly and almost all their time was spent collecting fuel.

About midday the men came out and ate their sandwiches round the fire. Mr Candlin was so grave that the boys did not dare to ask him how the work was going; and they were disappointed when the men returned to the tunnel without even mentioning what they had found. Now that they realized they were in for another spell of waiting, they felt that all the excitement had gone out of the adventure. The bright clear morning had turned to a dull afternoon, and the wind seemed to find out even their little sheltered corner. The sun began to dip and the short winter day wore away and grew cold. They grew tired of collecting the quick-burning stalks and let the fire go out. Dick began to feel weary of waiting, and wished that he was back in the colliery. Even the pony hung its head and looked despondent.

Then when it was already growing grey, and the weak and watery sun was almost down, the door was thrust open, and Mr Fairless came out and called them.

'Come on, my bonny lads! By sangs, you must both be tired to death of waiting for us. Mind, I'm not so sure that you should come in after all.'

'Why, Dad?'

'I think you might get a bit of a shock. Have you ever seen a skeleton, either of you?'

'No, Dad.'

'No, Mr Fairless.'

'Are you sure that you'd like to see one? You won't be frightened?'

'No, Dad.'

'No, Mr Fairless.'

'Now think it over. Do you really want to come in?'

'Yes, Dad.'

'Yes, Mr Fairless.'

'You'd make a good chorus, you two. Right. Now this is what I want you to do. Take one quick look, and then come straight out. Then if you don't feel too frightened, come in again and take in everything that Mr Candlin tells you.'

They followed him in, and as soon as they entered Dick felt his heart pounding with the same kind of excitement that he had felt when he had first gone down the staple. The tunnel was short, but it was very dark. At the end of it they came to a little chamber, just high enough for the men to stand upright in. In the middle stood the now lid-less coffin, and behind the coffin Mr Candlin with a hurricane lamp lifted high. Dick could hardly recognize him. His face was grimy, and the long ears looked more gnome-like than ever. Kit had once told him that you could raise the Devil if you went to the top of the hill in the dark, and the possibility that Mr Candlin might be Satan himself made him momentarily frightened. He looked down into the coffin, and there, looking very white in the blackness of the chamber, was the skeleton, with a discoloured skull lying on its side as if it had been twisted that way; and as

Mr Candlin moved his lamp the grinning skull seemed
almost to come to life.

He drew his breath in sharply; then Mr Fairless put a
strong hand on his shoulder, turned him and pushed him
and Peter out into the open air.

Mr Fairless let them breathe the clear air for a while,
and then he looked closely at them both.

'Have you had enough, lads? Do you think you can
face it again?'

'Do you want to, Dick?' asked Peter.

'Yes,' replied Dick. He was not sure, but he had been
brought up not to be a coward. 'Do you?'

'I do if you do.'

'Come on then, lads. But take your time. The air is a
bit foisty in there. Ready? Keep behind me, and see if
you can take in what Mr Candlin tells you.'

'That's a pair of stout fellows,' said Mr Candlin, smiling,
and Dick noticed with relief that he looked more like himself now. He had stood his lamp, too, on the corner of the
coffin and the skull seemed to have lost its sinister look.

He stood tight up against Peter, and the familiar sound of Mr Candlin's voice and the friendly pressure of his friend's arm dispelled the last traces of his panic.

'There you are, boys. Take a good look. We are the first human beings to see this man since he was buried here – how many years ago, would you say, Flem? – perhaps fifteen hundred years. And he's lying here just as he was put into the ground, with that big shield on his chest. And there's his dagger, see, lying across his thigh-bones, and that dark thing at his shoulder is his brooch, the brooch he used to fasten his cloak with.'

'Has the cloak disappeared?' asked Peter.

'Yes, all his clothes have rotted away, and so has the wooden shaft of his spear. But you can still see the spearhead. See it? There, just above his right shoulder. And there's the urn that may have been full of food for him. We'll find out later what's in it. You see he's been laid in his grave with weapons ready and his clothes on and food at hand for him – all ready for him when he entered on his new life.'

'But who was he, Mr Candlin?'

'I think he was an Anglo-Saxon chieftain. Somebody great who ruled some tribe or other living here in the fifth or sixth century perhaps ... do you know what I mean when I talk about centuries?'

'Yes, sir.'

'He must have been a great man or he would not have been given a fine tomb like this. But take a good look, boys. You're seeing something that you'll never see again.'

'Are you going to take him away, Mr Candlin?'

'Yes, we'll have to move all the things – coffin, bones and everything.'

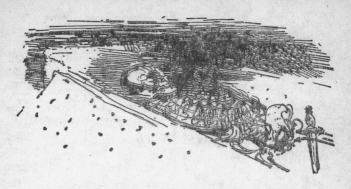

'And will this place be filled in again?'

'Yes, that will be your dad's next job.'

'Will you get any money for this?'

'Not really, Richard. Do you mean, will I sell these things?'

'Yes.'

'No, they're not for sale. But I'll get something better than money out of them.'

Dick was about to ask him what it was that was better than money when Mr Fairless broke in.

'I'll get the pony harnessed, Mark. The boys had better stay here as long as they can . . . Take it all in, boys. This is your last look.'

The boys looked for a few minutes in silence. Then Mr Fairless came back. They put the lid on the coffin, locked up the tunnel and started for home.

He had to tell his father and mother where he had been. They listened to him incredulously; and when he came to the skeleton his mother could not contain herself. 'A skeleton!' she said in a scandalized voice. 'What on earth has Flem Fairless been thinking about to show things like that to young lads? It's enough to give a bairn nightmares for the rest of his life.'

But Dick did not have a nightmare. On the contrary: when at school and in the street he was stopped and asked about his adventure with Mr Candlin he felt more important than he had ever been in all his life. More than that, Mr Candlin had shown him that this little corner of the world in which he and his father and all their friends lived, possessed secrets and wonders that he had never dreamt about.

13

Defeat

Meanwhile conditions grew more and more difficult for the strikers, and it became harder for them to keep well-fed and warm. When the shortage of fuel grew serious the men from both the tents and the streets began to raid the abandoned drift in the Rushy Field. In the darkness the boards were secretly removed, and in twos and threes the men worked the drift. It was dangerous work, for they had to find their own timber for the roof, and the coal they won was of very poor quality. Yet it was better than nothing, and night after night small parties entered the drift and filled their bags and barrows, and then before morning, covered up their traces and replaced the barricade.

One night Dick found himself involved in this work. When he came home his father was talking about him.

'Surely he's big enough now, Hetty. He isn't a baby. After all he's getting on for thirteen now.'

'What happens if he gets caught?'

'He'll take no harm. It's not as if we were asking him to commit a crime.'

'I still think he's too young to get mixed up in affairs like this.'

'What is it, Da?' asked Dick.

'We want you to do a little job, Dicky. It's our turn to work the drift with Billy Kelly – that's Kit and me. Billy's lad keeps an eye on the bottom of the field, and Old Simey usually watches the top of the lonnen for us. But Simey's a bit off colour, and we want somebody to take his place.'

'I can do that, Da.'

'Mind, you'll have to stop up till two in the morning, and you'll be all by yourself.'

'Doesn't matter, Da. I'm not frightened. I wasn't frightened when I saw that skeleton. And I don't get tired.'

'Yes, but what will you be like in the morning?' asked his mother.

'I'll be all right, Ma. Honest, I never get tired.'

'Then listen, and take everything in. Just sit behind the stone wall at the top of the field and keep an eye on anybody coming up the lonnen. If you see anybody that looks suspicious, nip back to the drift and give us the tip.'

'Have I to come in, Da?'

'Aye, but you won't have to come in very far. Mind, don't shout and yell and let everybody know what's up. Just tell us quietly, and we'll put the muggie out. Do you think you can manage?'

'Easy, Da.'

'That's a good lad. Wrap yourself up and . . . give the lad some bait, Hetty. Now as soon as you're ready, Dick, off you pop, and I'll come up just after two, and tell you when to come home.'

At the top of the field where the lonnen or lane entered it there was little shelter but the dry-stone wall that Mr Ullathorne had mentioned, but it was enough to keep the wind off, and Dick was not uncomfortable. Besides, he was in high feather at being entrusted with his task. He saw himself as a sentinel, and the lonnen was a frontier pass that he had to guard with all his attention and vigilance.

It was a mysterious night, still and full of secrets. The sky was unevenly covered with cloud, and behind the cloud moved a full moon, now completely hidden, now promising to emerge. Its full light filtered through the clouds and bathed the landscape in an even and revealing greyness. Now and then a sheep coughed, and a disturbed bird fluttered in the dry, bare hedge; and in the distance the lights of other collieries glowed like faint yellow constellations.

Dick felt no sense of fear. He felt rather a quickening of the senses, a thrill at being alone with the night for the first time. He felt it vibrating on his ear drums like the twanging of a bow, and under this vibration he picked out the tiny nocturnal sounds – a little runnel of water dropping down a roadside sink, the subdued *pu-we* of a restless lapwing, the sound of a goods train trundling slowly across country; and sometimes the machinery of some distant colliery would give a great sigh as if it had grown tired at last of hauling and delivering coal, and wanted to rest, as everyone else was resting.

Presently the far-off cathedral bell sounded midnight. The strokes advanced across the bare landscape, reached him and passed on; and the stillness seemed to deepen. Then, just when he was beginning to feel the cold closing in upon him, two figures appeared. They rounded the bend of the lane, reached the stile, and paused there to look at the field with its rows of tents that lay below them. From his shelter behind the wall Dick recognized one of them; it was Wanless, the Overman. The other was a stranger.

'Now then, Wanless,' the stranger said, 'just point out to me where that drift lies.'

'On the far side of the tents. But it's no good just walking through them. The dogs will give us away, for a start.'

'Which way should we go then?'

'Best work our way round the top. Mind, I'm bound to say that I don't fancy this job. Spying isn't my line. These fellows can be rough. I've found that out to my cost.'

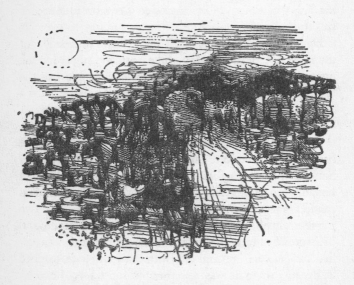

'I don't want any violence, but what I do want is names. Mr Sleath is certain that these men are working the drift under cover of darkness, and it's my job to provide him with evidence. They have no right to the drift, and anyone I can report working there will serve a stiff sentence.'

'Ah, now that's a different matter. If there's anybody working there, they'll have to come out sooner or later for something or other.'

'Will you be able to recognize them in this light?'

'I'll have a try.'

'Come on then.'

They moved off, and Dick, his heart beating fast with the urgency of the situation, waited till they were out of sight, and then ran like a hare through the lines of the tents, and splashed his way into the drift. He bumped his head on the roof, and felt the rusty pit water wetting his feet, but all this was forgotten in his anxiety to save his father. Fortunately the men were working at a stall not too far from the mouth. He saw them as soon as he rounded the first bend, and when they saw him they put out the light.

'What is it, Dick?'

'Mr Wanless and another man. Get out quick.'

They left their tools, hurried out without re-erecting the barricade, and threw themselves flat in the low ditch behind the sycamores. They were just in time, for no sooner had they concealed themselves than they saw the two men cautiously approaching the mouth of the drift. The two intruders took up a position opposite the entrance and prepared to wait; but after a while, being apparently satisfied that the drift was empty, they lit a lamp, approached it, looked round for signs of its being worked, ventured in, and came out with a shovel.

'Is your name on that, Da?'

'Thank God, it isn't. But just keep quiet, hinny. I think they'll move off soon.'

He was right. The men did not stay much longer. As the cathedral bell struck two, they moved away and disappeared over the brow of the hill.

'Well, Kit,' said Mr Ullathorne, when they were sure

they were safe, 'if I'm not mistaken that's the last bag of coal we'll get out of there. Mark my words, she'll be boarded up tomorrow, and there'll be a bobby here every night from now on. But we would have been in Queer Street if it hadn't been for our little Dick, wouldn't we?'

'Well done, kidder,' said Kit. 'You deserve a medal, lad.'

They all went home to bed, and Dick dreamt all night that he was guarding a pass in the Khyber, and rolling down great lumps of coal upon a horde of tribesmen, every one of whom was the spitting image of the Overman Wanless.

The boarding-up of the drift, which took place as Mr Ullathorne had foretold, was the beginning of many disasters for the strikers. The next was the ending of the strike pay. The strike had already lasted longer than had been anticipated, and the Union funds were exhausted. Then the women, who had tried their best to pay their way, had to pocket their pride and go begging to the shop-keepers for credit which was only rarely granted. The men took to raiding potato and turnip clamps, venturing far afield to cover up their traces. They poached rabbits and hares, collected nettles for soup, and took to smoking dried coltsfoot leaves; but most of what they collected went to their children. Fathers and mothers began to starve. Their complexions grew pale and drawn, their arms and legs thin and bony; and as their strength failed, so their hope and their courage dwindled.

In the end even the weather failed them. The mild days of that surprising winter gave way first to rain, then to cold east winds, then to snow. The winds that had seemed to sleep now awoke, and rode in savagely across the open landscape, tearing the weak canvas of the tents, and bringing in their wake the heavy wet snow that settled on the bleak hillside.

Of all these hardships Dick had noticed little. He was young, and life was exciting. School, play, the freedom of the fields, adventures with Peter, and evenings at the Fairlesses' – all these things had filled his days with interest. But when the bad weather came and confined his father and Kit and him to the cold tent, he began to see how much his parents were suffering; and it seemed to him that if only Mr Sleath knew how much they were having to undergo he would soon change his mind and let them go back to their homes. Suddenly he made up his mind that since Mr Sleath would not come to Branton to see for himself the distress of his men, he would go and tell him about it.

He told no one of his decision, but set off alone for Sion House. He had no difficulty in finding it. The events of that memorable evening when he had brought Mr Sleath home were too vivid for him to make mistakes; but as soon as he had passed the gate and entered the drive he felt his courage leaking away. The unfamiliarity of his surroundings daunted him. Impressive by night, the ugly house looked forbidding by day, and over it lay a silence unlike the clatter and activity of the colliery streets. If only the old deaf servant had appeared Dick might have gone up to him, but he did not dare walk unaccompanied up to the great sombre entrance and ring the bell. What would happen if there were new servants in the house? How could he explain what right he, a poor miner's son, had to come knocking on a wealthy man's door and asking for an interview?

Then as he hesitated, partly hiding behind a rhododendron bush, and partly hoping some friend might see him, he saw the trap being led by a strange groom to the great front door. The door itself opened, Mr Sleath got in and touched the pony into a trot. As it drew near Dick wondered if he dare run out of his hiding place and stop it; but his fear of the new groom and of Mr Sleath's stern face kept him back. It was only after the trap had passed him that he found his voice.

'Mr Sleath!' he cried; but Mr Sleath did not hear him. With the set, pre-occupied look of a man who is listening to nothing but his own thoughts, he drove on through the gate and out of hearing. Looking round, Dick saw the groom staring at him, and heard him whistle for a dog. He took to his heels and ran.

He never saw Mr Sleath again. In a few weeks the strike came to an end. The men gave in and accepted the owner's terms. The keys of their houses were restored to them, and the return to the colliery began.

To the returning families the two streets looked sad and neglected. Some of the windows had been broken, and gates and fencing had been stolen for fuel. The kitchen grates were rusty, and the uneven stone slabs of the bare kitchen floors were damp and sweaty. Wall-paper hung in shreds where furniture had been dragged out in haste, and the rooms smelt of mice. But the women were overjoyed to be back in their homes, and they went to work with a will. The rooms were dried out and began to take on their familiar homely smells; and all up and down the streets could be heard the sounds of the 'poss-sticks' drumming on the bottom of the washing tubs, and the water splashing over the grimy yards. The women ran out their clothes

lines, and hung out their long-neglected washing. The hawkers, the pedlars, the beggars, the order-men – all returned; and all the varied life of the streets sprang up again.

From the safe distance of his home in Durham Mr Sleath watched all these things. He watched the men settling back to their jobs, the women restoring their homes, the pit itself gathering life. He left the colliery in peace for a fortnight. Then, when he was certain that he was the complete master of the situation, he played his last card.

He was determined that never again would he allow his pit or any other pit, if he could help it, to be brought to a standstill by the men whom he suspected as the ringleaders of the strike. He made a list of these ringleaders, and gave orders that they were to be not only dismissed but black-listed. Every colliery in the country was given their names, and advised never, on any account, to employ them.

14

Dick Goes to Work

A few days later Mr Ullathorne was given his notice, and five others, including Peter's father and Mr Tredennick, were dismissed with him. A wave of anger swept through the colliery when the news was announced, but even Mr Ullathorne's most loyal friends knew that the dismissals would have to be accepted as one of the consequences of the defeat. Another strike was out of the question. It would lead only to further disaster.

'This could hardly have come at a worse time,' said Mr Ullathorne. 'Just when we are struggling to get on our feet again. But it's no good crying over spilt milk. I don't regret what I've done, and I'd do it again tomorrow if I had to.'

'It's a mercy that they've kept Kit on,' said his wife. 'His bit of money will come in very useful.'

'And what about me?' said Dick. 'I'm big enough to start work. I've heard them say that they want a lot of lads at the colliery. Can I start?'

'God forbid!' cried his mother.

'Stop at school, bonny lad,' said his father, 'and enjoy the sunshine for a bit longer. I'm sure to get a job at Evenside or Quaking Moor. They tell me they're crying out for men there.'

Mr Ullathorne had every right to be optimistic. The

coal trade was beginning to boom. New orders were coming in and new shafts were being sunk. As he tramped with his mates over the fells to Evenside, he felt confident they would be taken on. They were all men in the prime of their powers, fine hewers of coal. There were no better workmen in the country.

But Evenside did not want them. Neither did Quaking Moor, Nesh, Lambton Fell or Lowside. Wherever they went they received the same treatment.

'We don't want you here. We don't want any trouble-makers. The best thing for you fellows is to clear off the premises as quick as you can. There's nothing for you here.'

Everywhere they went, they were turned away. They were blacklisted, and their only hope was to seek work in another county.

'I doubt we'll have to pack up and shift, Hetty,' said Mr Ullathorne when he realized that, go where he might, there was no work for him.

'I dinna fancy going among strange folks, Davy, at my time of life, but I suppose we'll have to do it.'

'There's nothing else for it, Hetty.'

'Why don't you give them another name when you ask for work, Da?' asked Dick.

'What's that, hinny?'

'Why don't you call yourself Addison or Williams or something, and say that you live at the Groyne or Skilling-ton? Nobody would know, would they?'

'Nay, lad, David Ullathorne I was born, and David Ullathorne I shall be till the end of my days. Nay, there's just one way out, Hetty.'

'What's that?'

'We'll have to change our minds about Dicky. Aye, lad,

you'll have to help us out for a bit.'

'Do you mean I'll have to start work?'

'That's it.'

'Will they take him on, Davy?'

'Here's our Kit. Ask him. Kit, do you think they'll take our Dick on at the colliery?'

'Sure to. They're crying out for lads in our pit. They'll take him like a shot.'

'There we are then. Kit, will you take him down to the offices and get his name put down?'

'That I will ... So, tha's ganna be a man at last, eh kidder?'

'I'll be a hewer before you,' replied Dick with spirit.

'A hewer? That's a good 'un! Tha couldn't hew the skin off a rice pudding.'

'I know one that will not be pleased,' said Mrs Ulla-thorne, 'and that's your mother, Davy.'

'If she doesn't like it, she'll have to lump it. Anyhow you can't keep a lad sitting on his backside for ever. Come on, Dick, my lad, and see if we can find a pit bottle for thee.'

When old Mrs Ullathorne heard the news, she decided to make it quite clear that she did not approve. It was not in her nature to interfere in the affairs of others. Indeed, it was only on rare occasions that she left her home, even to visit her own son. When she ventured out into the colliery streets she still moved among them as a stranger, shrinking from the ugliness and the mud.

Her visits, though infrequent, always put Mrs Ulla-thorne in a fluster. She knew that the older woman was of different mettle; she was afraid of the pride and the reti-cence that were so much unlike the easy-going ways of the

colliery. Old Mrs Ullathorne, in her turn, never unbent, never invited intimacy. She declined the rocking-chair before the fire, preferring a hard chair near the door. Hetty, too, chose a hard chair, and waited for the old woman to begin.

'Is David in?' she asked. She never called him Davy. She disliked shortened names.

'He's gone off to see about getting himself some work n the turnip-fields.'

'Has Richard gone with him?'

'He's gone off to see about a pair of pit ... a pair of boots.'

'I hear that he has been taken on at the colliery.'

'Yes, he has,' replied Mrs Ullathorne. The older woman never used dialect, and Hetty tried hard not to use it in reply. The consequence was that her speech became forced and unnatural.

'Do you think that you are doing the right thing by the boy?'

'We haven't any option. David cannot get a job for love nor money. Somebody's got to addle a few pence.'

Hetty soon forgot her resolve to speak politely. The old woman nettled her, and the more nettled she became the rougher her speech grew.

'I thought your older son was working.'

'What – our Kit? What he brings in winna keep us in shoe-leather.'

'At the same time you shouldn't sacrifice your younger son. Do you and David value the boy as you should?'

'He's my lad. I know him as well as the next.'

'Then you should realize that he has brains.'

'And what good's brains at a time like this?'

'They're worth more than you think. It's my opinion that Richard has a future, but not if he goes into the pit.'

'His da's in the pit and his brother's in the pit, and I cannot see that it's done them any harm.'

'It hasn't done them any good, and you should be the first to see that, particularly at this time. I know you won't take my advice, but I think he ought to stay at school.'

'And what are we supposed to do for money?'

'People can always manage if they want to manage.'

'It's all very well for them that never has to worry about the next penny. There are some folks that have plenty in their pocket, and never know the meaning of want . . .'

If she finished her sentence the old woman did not hear it. Old Mrs Ullathorne always avoided ugly scenes. She never stooped to brawling; that was an indignity she left to commoner folk. Before Hetty had finished her sentence, she had opened the door, descended the steps, and was on her way home.

Mr Ullathorne valued his mother's opinion, but he did not consult her. Discussion between the two was not easy, for there always stood between them the barrier of her secret wealth, and he was too proud and independent to mention that subject. He went ahead with his own plan and put Dick to work. The boy was still not quite thirteen when his schooldays came to an end.

It was a bright cold morning when he left for his first shift. The starlings were whistling on the roofs of the colliery houses when he set out, and he never forgot the clear penetrating sound of their calls as he walked down the street. He felt awkward in his first pit clothes, in the jacket that was far too big for him, and the heavy new-studded boots that clattered on the uneven pavements. His white bait-poke was slung around his left shoulder, and his jacket pocket bulged with his pit bottle. He felt that everyone was looking at him as he trudged with Kit past the depots, along the line, across the pit yard, and into the lamp-cabin.

'What do you want, Dicky, a left-handed lamp or a reet-handed one?' said the lamp-cabin man, laughing as

Dick faltered, failing to see the joke.

'They tell me,' said another man, 'that they've given tha a job cleaning the windows down pit.' But Kit looked after him, helping him to laugh at the men's chaff, and making sure that he learnt the ropes.

'Try not to swing your lamp, Dicky, when you get inbye,' he said. 'If you do, you'll dazzle the fellow that's walking behind you.'

All the men who were to go down the pit on this shift were gathered together at the pithead. As they waited for the cage, they seemed to Dick to grow quiet. There was plenty of noise all round them – the turning of the pulley wheels, the knocking and bumping of machinery, the upward and downward thrusting of the pumps, and the far-away sound of the rapper stopping or releasing the unseen

cages; but the men seemed to be composing themselves for the quietness of the mine. At last it was their turn to ride, and Dick watched the rope slipping upward, the cage chains appear, and then the cage itself. As the men entered the cage they sat down on their 'unkers'; they believed they could better take the shock of any unexpected bump or jolt if they were crouching. When they were all in, the gates closed with a clang, and the cage was rapped away. The pulleys began to spin, the cage fell, at first gently, then rapidly until the sides of the shaft down which it slid were all one blur, and Dick's stomach rose. He had the strange sensation of going not down, but up; but before he had time to realize fully what was happening to him, the cage had stopped, the doors were flung open, and he was at the bottom of the shaft. He had entered his new world.

He was to work first of all as a trapper, and all he had to do was to stay by a wooden door that closed one of the galleries, to open it for any traffic that might want to pass, and close it after it had gone through. It was not an exciting task, but someone had to do it, for on the correct opening and shutting of the trap-door depended the primitive ventilation system of the pit.

But it was a lonely job. He had to sit by himself, with no light except the faint gleam of his pit-lamp, for long silent hours when the traffic was slack; and sitting there, he had strange fancies. Sometimes he thought he saw figures coming towards him out of the darkness, and he had to take up his lamp and shine it into the shadows to reassure himself that there was nothing there. All the features of this new strange world impressed themselves upon him – the uneven slope of the wagon-way, the pools of muddy water between the short sleepers, the black and brilliant sides of the seam.

His first day seemed endless. When he felt that half of the shift was over, he ate his bait and drank some of the cold tea his mother had put in his pit bottle; but when he asked the time he found that only a quarter of the shift had passed. By the time he came to the end of his first day he was aching with hunger, and as he stepped out of the cage the upper world seemed something he had not seen for a year.

Dick worked as a trapper for a month. Then another boy came to take his place, and Dick, to his great joy, was sent to help Mr Turnbull, who was in charge of the pit ponies. Alec Turnbull was as fine a master as the boy could have wished for, a proud, conscientious man who took great pains with his work, and kept his stables as clean as his own house.

'Because my ponies are underground,' he would say, 'that's no reason why they shouldn't be looked after properly. This is how I look at it, Dick – when ponies never see the light of day they deserve the best, and nothing but the best, and that's what I try to give them.'

He was no empty talker. He always made good what he said, and he spared neither himself nor anybody else to make his ponies comfortable. He prided himself on their condition, and he and Dick examined every pony at least once a day so that no cut or bruise or ailment went undetected. All the rough putters feared him, for he had beaten with his own fists many a man who had dared to maltreat his ponies; but they respected him.

In Alec's company Dick's schooldays fell rapidly behind him. For six days out of seven he trudged to the pithead, entered the cage, and descended into the pit, only to ascend when most of the daylight was spent. He was not discontented. He often recalled the times when as a boy he had wakened at the sound of the caller and felt envious of the men going to work. Now he was one of them. He sat on his 'unkers' with them, waiting for his turn in the cage. He had his own pit bottle and bait-poke, and his own work. He sat among the men at bait-time and was accepted as one of them. In the evenings when the shift was over, he washed himself in the zinc bath before the fire, and ate his pot-pie, and if it was still light enough, went out to watch the men playing quoits or hand-ball. Then at the end of the week he drew his pay and handed it over to his mother.

He never saw Mr Bradwell now; yet he did not lose his love of learning and reading, and always preserved within himself that part of him that his teacher and his grandmother had recognized. It was a curiosity, a love of something far and uplifting, a hunger and an appetite to which he could not give a name, but which nourished him without unsettling him.

Mr Turnbull was a good friend to him. He was no great reader, but he had one or two books that he cherished. His favourite was a little book of poetry called *The Wild Hills of Waley*, and when the pair of them were sitting having their bait, and the conversation came round to books, he would often quote from it.

'Now there's a book you would like reading, Dick. It was poor Harry Clennel that wrote that, and when I was a lad I used to hear him talking about the Hills of Waley.'

'Did you really know him?'

'Aye, he was a friend of my father.'

'And are they real hills?'

'Real? I should think they are. I've walked over them many a time.'

' "Wherever I wander, wherever I roam," Harry used to say, and you can see the lines written down in his book, "The Wild Hills of Waley will still call me home." '

'That's lovely, isn't it, Alec?'

'Aye, he was a bonny good hand at things like that.

> The rowan tree grows by the old cottage door,
> And the blaeberry grows on the desolate moor.'

'I would like to see them hills some day.'
'And one of these fine days we will see them, Dick.'
'Is it a long way?'
'It's a tidy stride. It's a canny distance. But one of these fine days we'll get there.'

There was little real likelihood of their ever doing so, for holidays were a luxury no pitman could ever think of; but to Dick it was a pleasure merely to dream of walking on those hills, treading through the heather and the clumps of blaeberry, and repeating the musical lines of the dead poet.

While they worked Alec talked to the boy, and told him stories of his own early life, when his father had been a shepherd on the far fells of Northumberland. He had worked first of all as a stable-boy, then a groom, and then had drifted to the pits and become a horse-keeper. He had a fund of stories, and as they sat having their bait together, he would tell Dick anecdotes of ponies he had known.

'I once had a bonny little pony, called Roanie. He would do anything for a lump of sugar, and you could guarantee that whatever he was up to, you could bring him to a full stop if you just said, "Sugar, Roanie". Wherever he was he would stop dead in his tracks. Once we were all on strike, ten years back and maybe more, and I fetched all the ponies up and put them in the colliery field. You should have seen them, Dick. They were just like bairns at a chapel treat. But we had some rough young lads in the colliery then, and they wouldn't keep off the ponies. They would keep on trying to ride them. Why, one day, I saw one of these young lads, the worst of the bunch, and he was on Roanie, slashing away at him and getting him to gallop. "Right, my boyo," I said to myself, "I'll fix you!" And just as he was coming past I shouted, "Sugar, Roanie!" Roanie stopped as if he'd been shot, and that fellow went over his neck like a stone out of a catapult.'

He would smile as he told stories like this, but when he told of the death of ponies in accidents in the mine his eyes would grow clouded. He was deeply fond of ponies, and taught Dick how to like them and care for them.

'Try not to get too fond of them, lad,' Mr Turnbull would say to him; but it was more than Dick could do to obey him. His favourite was a little black mare with a queer-shaped splash of white not quite in the middle of her brow; and when her shift was over she would come straight to Dick and put her head right over his shoulder. Her name was Bonny, and Dick adored her. He often thought that if ever he became rich, the first thing he would do would be to bring her out of the pit and let her live all her life in a proper field and a proper stable.

Dick's was a small world, but he found more satisfaction in his work than he had hoped. He enjoyed working with Mr Turnbull, and still spent a great deal of time with Peter and Mr Fairless. They no longer lived in Cobden Terrace, and were poorer now; but Mr Fairless was a capable man, and picked up enough money here and there to keep Peter at school. He thought the world of the two boys. It was he who took Dick for the first time into the cathedral at Durham, and at week-ends he would take them on foot to places hitherto unknown to them – strange earthworks on the fells, an abbey hidden away in the woods, an ancient church on the fringe of some colliery. To Dick these things were a revelation. They were part of a new and wonderful world, the existence of which he had never even dreamt of.

For Mr Ullathorne, however, the future was full of foreboding. He too remained unemployed, and though, especially as the days lengthened, he found enough work in the fields to keep going, he was unhappy. He was at heart a pitman, happy only when he was at work in the pit. He stayed at Branton only for the sake of his wife, who could not bear the thought of leaving her neighbours and going among strange people, but he felt that sooner or later, if fortune did not change, he would have to leave the county.

For a while they were allowed to stay in Chapel Row because the boys were at work, but when, like Mr Fairless, they were compelled to move into a rented cottage on the outskirts of the colliery, Mr Ullathorne realized at last that Mr Sleath was determined never to forgive him. He began to lose heart and his health began to suffer.

His father's ill-health and the knowledge that sooner or later he would have to say good-bye to Peter and Mr Fairless troubled Dick and clouded his happiness.

15

'Till We Meet Again'

Mr Fairless and Mr Ullathorne were not the only ones to suffer from Mr Sleath's malice. None of the blacklisted men could find work in the county, and one by one they had to leave. After a while Mr Fairless, Mr Tredennick and Mr Ullathorne were the only ones left. Of these Mr Ullathorne was the most fortunate. He had two sons to help him; but for Mr Fairless the situation was almost unbearable. Dick therefore was dismayed but not surprised when he heard his father say one night, 'Have you heard the latest about Flem Fairless and Jo Tredennick?'

'No. What have they been up to?'

'You'll be surprised when I tell you. They're off to Australia.'

'Never!'

'It's gospel. They've booked their passages. They're selling up on Wednesday and they're off on Sunday.'

'Mind that's a decision to make.'

'Aye, and for two pins I'd be off with them,' said Mr Ullathorne, and for a moment Dick thought that he was serious, that after all he might not be separated from his friends, but his mother's reply dashed his hopes.

'Dinna talk like that, for heaven's sake, Davy. You put me all in a flutter. Whatever do they expect to do in Australia?'

'They can get work. They've made sure of that.'

'And when do you say they are setting off?'

'They're catching the night train from Durham on Sunday.'

'Is anybody seeing them off?'

'Anybody? I'll lay a pound to a pinch of salt the whole of Branton will be there to see them off.'

Mr Fairless had been thinking for some time of leaving the country, and had often spoken about it; but Dick had no idea that he was so near to making a decision. He knew that he would miss them deeply, because they had come to be his best companions. There was no one else in the colliery, except Mr Turnbull, who could inspire him as Peter's father had. There was no one who could fill the gap their going would leave.

It was with a heavy heart that he walked into Durham on Sunday evening and climbed the long winding slope to the station. He was not the only one who had come to say good-bye. The station was crowded with well-wishers. Most of them had taken platform tickets and had gone through the barrier; the rest crowded outside the railings and clambered on benches and boxes and barrows to call out their farewells to their friends. The hollow station resounded with their calls.

'All the best, Flem! All the best, Jo!'

'Take care, Bessie! Take care, Sarah!'

'We'll be thinking about you.'

'God bless you all!'

The two men went backwards and forwards shaking hands across the railings. They were both proud men. They had endured poverty and victimization for their principles, but their spirit was unbroken. They both held

themselves erect, with their courageous and defiant heads
thrown back a little. The heart-felt good-byes and the
long handshakes moved them, but they hid their feelings.
The two women wept quietly as they embraced their
neighbours, making a show of declining the little presents
that were pressed upon them. The children sat on the low
straw basses that contained their luggage, and looked incredulously at the scene around them. They were stiff,
and weary of waiting. Dick had gone through the barrier
to say good-bye to Peter. They hardly knew what to say
to each other, and in the pauses in their conversation Dick
could hear the gas hissing in the jets over the platform, and
the noise of a man testing the wheels of some carriage in a
near-by siding. The cold air of the northern evening began
to move in upon the open platform.

Suddenly a bell rang, a signal went down, and the crowd
began to stir. Out of the darkness came the lights and then
the noise and then the bulk of the huge express. It seemed
to be bearing down upon the station with ferocious speed
as though it meant to plough its way through the crowd,
and the first carriages slid swiftly past; but at last it
slackened speed, it halted, it stopped, and all up and down
its length doors were flung open. Mr Fairless and Mr
Tredennick and their families climbed abroad and a dozen
hands passed their luggage up to them. Dick could see
them through the steamy windows lifting their basses and
their flimsy parcels on to the luggage racks. Then they
came to the windows to take their last farewells. The doors
began to slam, and a whistle was heard; and at that moment someone began to sing –

God be with you till we meet again,

and at once the hymn was taken up by every voice, and all the noises of the departing train – the banging of the doors, the whistle, the sudden snort of steam – all were drowned by the fervent singing of a hundred voices –

> God be with you till we meet again,
> By His counsels guide, uphold you,
> With His sheep securely fold you;
> God be with you till we meet again . . .

The train jerked a little. The carriages moved forward in short thrusts, then slid smoothly away. Carriage followed carriage till there was no more to follow. All that was visible was the retreating light of the train, the glare of its fire on the twisting cloud of steam and smoke, and the waving hands from the windows.

There was one man on the platform saying good-bye to Mr Fairless who was not from Branton. It was Mr Candlin. Dick had not noticed him till now but as the crowd turned to go through the barrier he recognized him and smiled.

'Hello, there,' said Mr Candlin, when they had passed through the gate. 'Richard Ullathorne – that's who it is, isn't it?'

'Yes, Mr Candlin.'

'I thought I recognized you – my little fellow excavator. Have you got over the shock of seeing that skeleton yet?'

'It wasn't much of a shock, sir. I've seen worse than that.'

'How's that? Are you working? Are you in the pit?'

'Yes, sir.'

'What a pity! What a pity! Are you going to stay there?'

'I don't know, Mr Candlin.'

'Don't let it swallow you up, Richard. What's it that it says in the Bible – "Let not the flood sweep over me, or the pit close its mouth over me"? You're too bright to spend your life in darkness. You've got talents. Don't bury them. Don't hide your light under a bushel. And keep learning, Richard. Learning will never let you down.'

The next day, as if to underline all that Mr Candlin had said, an unusual piece of furniture was delivered to Mr Ullathorne's house. It was Mr Fairless's bureau, which he had not included in the sale. In the bureau was a letter:

Dear Dick

I know you have always had a fancy for this desk of mine. I've seen you casting an eye on it many a time. Well, now it's yours, Dick, and so is the pen that you'll find in the right-hand drawer. I know you will make good use of both of them, so God bless you.

Robert Flemington Fairless

It was the first piece of furniture that Dick had ever possessed. He put it in the bedroom he shared with Kit. At first, he had nothing to put in it, but he discovered in the covered market in Durham a second-hand stall where bargains could be picked up. It was mainly a tool stall, loaded with rusty hammers, old planes, screw-drivers and drills, with washers and bolts and nuts hanging from wires like strings of onions; but in one corner were piled dozens of dusty volumes, novels by forgotten authors, books of views and engravings, old hymn books, scientific hand-books and classical texts. To forage among these dusty piles was almost as grimy a task as sifting cinders on the Fiery Heap; but from this fusty collection he chose odd treasures, and stored them lovingly in his beloved bureau.

Often when his father and Kit sat in the kitchen talking their mysterious pit language, he went to the cold bed-room and pored with delight on the dog-eared dusty volumes he had bought with his own pennies. In the first few he had written –

Richard Ullathorne,
Morley Cottage,
Branton Colliery,
Co. Durham,
England,
Europe,
The Northern Hemisphere,
The World,
The Universe.

– but he soon regretted writing so much, and simply in-scribed the rest 'Richard Ullathorne'.

16

The Accident

Branton was in many respects an old-fashioned colliery. Mr Sleath had for years refused to make any improvements in the working conditions of the men. Most of the equipment was old and in poor condition; but rather than spend money on keeping his machinery in good order, he preferred to let it run till it broke down. Provided he made his fortune, and was able to salve his conscience by gifts now and then to chapels, he did not care what happened to his mine or to his successors.

Some time before Dick had left school, a law had been passed compelling all mine-owners to provide their pits with a second shaft. There had been several disasters and many lives had been lost in pits that only had one entrance and exit. Mr Sleath took very little notice, however, of the law. He made a show of starting on the work, but he had little intention of completing it. When Dick began work the new shaft was not even half sunk. It had not even reached the first seam.

Fortunately for him nothing serious happened to draw attention to the dangers of the situation. Day by day the single shaft with its old-fashioned machinery bore the brunt of the work. Day by day the old cages carried the men down and the coal up, and nothing happened to make the outside world realize the grave risks that Mr Sleath was compelling his workmen to take, every day of their waking lives. Nothing occurred to wake the conscience of the world outside Branton, until one fatal morning in September less than a year after the beginning of the strike.

September the sixteenth was a lovely day. It was Monday, and all the colliery, after its brief rest, was resuming the work of the week. The starlings whistled and swooped down for the crusts and bacon rinds thrown out on to the dry streets. Half a dozen mongrels played in and out of the drying posts. The first hawkers of the week were going up and down the streets uttering their long-drawn-out cries –

'Caller Herr'n! Caller Herr'n!'

'Sandy-stone and scoury-stone! Sandy-stone and scoury-stone!'

'Tubs to mend! Any tubs to mend!'

'Scissors-a-grind, scissors-a-grind!'

All up and down the rows could be heard the thumping of the poss-sticks in the poss-tubs as the women set about their washing. Washing lines were run out, and hung with white and coloured laundry that waved and stirred in the lovely September light.

The quiet morning was filled with the familiar sounds of the colliery, the barking of the dogs, the sound of hammering coming from the shops, the cries of the hawkers ... until just before noon a strange and unfamiliar sound was heard, a sound of large beams suddenly cracking and splitting, a tearing away of timber, a collapsing of bricks. To the incredulous eyes that turned towards the pithead, the pulleys, the stocks, all the pithead gear suddenly heeled and fell as if they were being sucked in and swallowed by the shaft, and over them rose a cloud of dust and dirt.

Man, woman and child ran as fast as they could to the pit-head; and there to their great horror they learnt that the shaft, the only shaft, had somehow caved in, and the only way in and out of the pit was blocked with more tons of wreckage and rubble than anyone dared to reckon.

By the evening everyone knew exactly what had happened, and had begun to fear the worst.

Branton's single shaft was not only a haulage shaft; that is, it was not used only for men and tubs. To it was also fixed the pumping machinery, the pump shaft being divided from the haulage shaft by no more than a series of flimsy partitions that ran for its own length. The massive pumping-engine rested on a big beam that was laid across the pit mouth, and it was this beam that had suddenly and without warning snapped. As the machinery fell, it carried with it all its gearing, and this great weight of metal in its descent ripped away the partitions and even the walling of the shaft. Beams, spars, machinery, girders and walling had all been carried to the bottom where they lay jammed together. More than that, a huge quantity of loose stone had been dislodged, and this, piling upon the debris, had completely sealed the shaft; and in the now inaccessible seams no less than two hundred men and boys were entombed. Among them were Kit and Dick.

Late that night almost all Branton gathered at the pit-head. The children, ignorant of the danger, played on the wagons and tubs that stood in the yard. The women stood in their shawls, very patient and showing no obvious signs of grief. Now and then one of the men who were left above would volunteer to be lowered into the shaft. A rope was slung over makeshift pulleys, and with his lamp strapped to him the volunteer descended; but the message that was brought back was always the same. The sides of the shaft had been almost ruined. It was rammed tight as if it had been plugged, and whoever tried to work there would be in constant danger from the rubble that continued to fall. While the men worked the women stayed on. Right through the night they remained near the pit yard, making short journeys back to their homes for food and drink, not for themselves, but for the men, and waiting patiently for the miracle to happen and for their men to emerge.

By this time the men below had recovered from the first shock of finding themselves entombed, and they had all collected in the Busty seam, which was the highest in the pit, and was fortunately connected with the lower seams by narrow ramps. All the men had managed to escape

through these narrow passages, but the ponies had been
abandoned.

Dick did not have time to worry about his own safety.
The sound of their whinnying drove everything else out
of his mind.

'Can't I go down and try and get some of them up,
Alec?' he pleaded. 'I'm certain I can get Bonny up the
ramp.'

'It's no use, lad. We've done as much as we can. They'll
settle down after a bit, and we'll get them out later. But
I'm not making fish of one and flesh of the other. Go and
sit a bit farther inbye and you won't hear them.'

Dick moved away. Once he thought wildly of going back himself and slaughtering Bonny painlessly so that he would not have to listen to her whinnying for him, but he had nothing with him but a pocket knife; and besides he knew that when it came to the point he would not be able to hurt her. He put his hands over his ears and moved farther inbye. When he came back after a while the whinnying had ceased. He did not dare to ask Alec what had happened.

Suddenly the silence and darkness filled him with fear and there came back to him that terror of the unknown that he had felt in the first few hours he had spent as a trapper. He moved more closely to his friend, who put his arm around him protectively.

'I doubt we'll never see the Wild Hills of Waley now, Alec,' he said sadly.

'Hout, man,' replied Alec, forcing a smile. 'We'll see them yet. And if we don't we'll see something just as good.'

'What's that?'

'Somebody will have to buy new ponies – that is, if anything happens to these,' he added, seeing a look of concern on Dick's face. 'That will mean a trip up the dale for somebody.'

'Will you go?'

'Both of us, lad, if I have anything to do with it.'

'Me?'

'Why not? You're as good a judge of ponies as anybody I've seen. We'll both have a trip up the dale.'

'What's it like up there?'

'Champion, Dick, champion. No smoke, no muck, and air like wine.'

'Do you think we'll get out of here, Alec?'

'Get out? Man alive, what's to stop us? What's today?
Monday? If we're not out of here by tomorrow night, I'll
eat my hat. Keep thy pecker up, Dick. We'll see the Wild
Hills of Waley yet.'

To the men, waiting in the gloom of the seam for a
sound from the rescue team which they knew would be
searching for them, every minute seemed an hour. They
found plenty to talk about. They were fond of 'cracking',
as they called it; but now as they cracked they listened.
They were listening for the noises of the search party, or
the noises of the rising waters, the sounds that would mean
life or death. Every now and then they would fall silent as
some new sound made itself heard, and then the quiet
conversation would begin again. Happily it was warm and

dry where they were, and the air was good. Once one of the boys fainted, but he was soon brought round, and showed no signs of serious weakness. On another occasion one or two of the chapel men began to pray, and a small group began on a hymn, but the rest of the men did not like it. They were a stoical band of men, and did not like giving way to any emotion.

The older men who had taken charge did not let the entombed men sit entirely idle. They did their best to keep them occupied; but after a while an apathy began to settle on the men. As Dick sat watching them he saw despair coming over them. The conversation flagged, and some of them lay down on the dusty ground, or propped themselves against the coal-face and closed their eyes. Then as he watched them he suddenly recognized an old man whom he had not previously seen. It was old Jossie Milburn; and with the recognition there flashed into his mind an idea that made him jump to his feet and hurry to find his brother.

'Kit,' he said, 'Jossie Milburn's here!'

'Who?'

'Jossie Milburn.'

'What about it?'

'It was Jossie that we stole the pick from. Has he always worked in this seam?'

'I couldn't say, lad. What's all the excitement for?'

'If he was in this seam last year, there might be a way out to the staple!'

'Lad, is it possible?'

'We should ask him, Kit.'

'Man alive, Dick, I never thought of it. Thank God for thy brains. Where is he?'

They found the old man sitting despondently with his back up against the coal-face. His eyes were closed, and his arms hung slack by his sides.

'How's tha gettin' on, Jossie?' said Kit.

'Not so bad, Kit, not so bad. But it looks black. I've worked in this seam for nigh on thirty years, and, by sangs, it looks as if I'm ganna finish here.'

'Don't say that, Jossie. Is this the seam you were in last year?'

'Last year? Aye, that was a bad year for me. Do you remember that day when I lost my pick? All the colliery was talking about it. Nay, I don't suppose you can remember it. That was a sign, Kit. I should have taken notice of that and knocked off work straight away. But I carried on hewing, and look where it's landed me.'

'Yes, but listen, Jossie – was it in this seam that you lost your pick? Was it here?'

'Not here, but I was in this seam. I was working right inbye, as far in as you could get. We used to call it the back o' beyond. I had the last cavil in that seam, and a terrible cavil it was. The divvel himself couldn't have got coals out of that place.'

'Could you find that place again?'

'Not from here. They closed her up when I came out. I should think they let the top down once I'd finished, because I can remember the Overman saying that they'd never try to get any more coal out of there. Man, it was a day's march from the shaft bottom. I used to be finished before I started.'

'Jossie, don't move from this place. I want to bring the Overman to have a few words with you.'

'What for? I've done nothing wrong, have I?'

'Just the opposite, Jossie. You may be the salvation of the lot of us.'

There was one Overman among the entombed men. It was Mr Blenkinsop, a staid, sensible man who was well liked, modest and good-living. Kit knew that he would get a hearing from him.

'Mr Blenkinsop, can you come over to where Jossie Milburn is for a minute?'

'Certainly.'

They moved over, and then Kit asked Jossie to withdraw with them a little so that they could talk without being overheard.

'What's all the mystery about, Kit?' asked the old man.

'I'll tell you. Jossie, can you tell Mr Blenkinsop where it was you were working when you lost your pick last year?'

'What's Mr Blenkinsop got to do with that?'

'Never mind. Just tell him.'

'Well, I will, for all the good it will do. I was along the first turning on the left off the main wagon-way, straight on past where the deputy used to keep his chest, then another turn to the left and up there as far as you can get. It was a day's march, I can tell you.'

'Do you know it, Mr Blenkinsop?'

'No, not as far as I can tell. Is that the place that I've heard called Lonnen End?'

'Aye, that's it.'

'Is it still open, Mr Blenkinsop?'

'Not now. I seem to remember being told when I came here that they'd closed that section. They let the top down.'

'Do you think it's badly blocked?'

'I couldn't say. But what are you driving at, lad?'

'Mr Blenkinsop, I don't want to raise any false hopes, but it's my belief that if we can get through to that cavil where Jossie used to work, we can get out.'

'Impossible, man, impossible.'

'It isn't. I've done it. What's more, there's two of us here that's done it. Me and our Dick. And I'll tell you how I can prove it. We were the ones that stole your pick.'

'What?'

'When we were just lads we went down the staple and got lost. We worked our way along to Lonnen End, and took your pick, Jossie, to help us to get out.'

'This beats everything! I've never heard, never, in all my born days ...'

'Kit,' said Mr Blenkinsop, 'there may be something in this, and there may not, but we've got to try it. I want the three of you to set off and see how far you can get to Lonnen End. But mind, not a word to anybody. I don't want to raise the men's hopes just to see them dashed. Slope off as quietly as you can, and let nobody see you.'

Jossie, Kit and Dick made off as inconspicuously as they could towards Lonnen End, and half an hour later they came upon the fall which, as the Overman had suspected, separated them from the old cavil.

'This is it, Dick,' said Kit. 'Go back and tell Mr Blenkinsop we've come up against the fall, but the wagon-way is still in good shape. Tell him he can bring a few tubs up, and there's room for about six men to work at once, clearing and filling.'

Eventually Mr Blenkinsop and his party assembled.

'Now look, lads,' he said, 'this is just a bare chance for us all. I'm fairly certain that behind that fall there's a way up to Lonnen End, and Kit says there's another way from there to the old staple that comes out behind Johnson's farm. He may be right and he may not. Don't expect too much. This fall may be a few yards thick, and it may be a hundred. Take your time, and for God's sake be careful. Put up plenty of timber wherever you can. The top's sure to be loose and she may cave in on you any minute. Remember, don't punish yourselves, and I'll fetch somebody to give you a spell. And not a word to anybody, mind.'

It was hard work. By now there was no food of any kind left, and nothing to drink except the brackish water brought up from the flooded seams. Many of the men had by this time been two days without sleep. In addition the air was bad, and the work discouraging. Wherever a section was cleared, earth and loose stone ran in like salt out of a cellar. Whatever parts of the roof remained unbroken cracked and gave alarmingly, and the men had to timber up with great care whenever they made an advance. When the first workers fell back, a second team took their place, pushed the work a little farther forward, and rested. The first team did another spell, and rested again. The second team, who had snatched a short sleep in the goaf, set to work once more ... and at last, more than sixty hours after the accident, they broke through.

They sent Dick through first. As soon as the hole was big enough for his thin body, he wriggled through, took a lamp and went ahead alone. As long as he could look back and see the light of Kit's lamp showing through the hole he was confident, but when he turned a corner and lost sight of it he felt fearful and alone. A few yards farther on a strange green glow made him jump, but he forced himself to go up to it and saw that the light came from a length of rotting phosphorescent timber. Then just beyond it he saw the cavil where Jossie had worked, the little cupboard-like hole cut into the coal-face, the timber, and a broken clay-pipe. He hurried back and told what he had seen.

'Well done, Dick,' said Mr Blenkinsop. 'Now we have a chance. Take a rest, men. I'm going ahead with Dick and Kit as soon as we can all get through, and then I'll tell you the next move. Lie down, lads. Take it easy for a bit, and try not to sweat, and don't waste your strength. We'll need all we have before we're out of this.'

Together the Overman and the two boys set off into the darkness, and after fifty yards they came to Lonnen End.

'There it is, Mr Blenkinsop. That's where I saw Jossie leave his pick,' said Kit. 'If we're where I think we are, we should come to a boarding in about a hundred yards. Keep on, Mr Blenkinsop. It's not bad going here. There she is – I can see her!'

'So can I,' cried Dick. 'This is the way, Mr Blenkinsop, I'm sure of it.'

'Can you get through that boarding easily?'

'The planks are rotten. Look, you can push them down. And look, Mr Blenkinsop, there's one of the chalk marks that we made to keep us on the right track. Would you believe it – it's still there! The others should be there as well, and they should take us right back to the staple.'

'That's evidence enough for me. But, wait – do you think this way has altered much?'

'I think the roof's lower,' said Dick. 'I think it was higher when we first came; and the sides seem to be more squeezed together.'

'That's just what I was afraid of. I have a feeling she may have closed in on us. But let's get back and tell the men where we stand now. It might not be long now afore we see the light of day.'

When he got back he wakened the men and told them what they had seen.

'And now,' he said, 'I'm proposing to tell all the men just what our chances are. Kit, go to the shaft bottom and tell them all to make their way here. We're not out of it yet, lads, and God alone knows what kind of trouble we'll run into afore we're finished. But God helps them that help themselves, and one thing's certain – if we lie down now, we're finished. How long is it, Kit, since the shaft got jammed?'

'About sixty hours.'

'Must be more than that. My guess is that it's nearer three days. We're all beginning to feel the worse for wear, and it's only natural. But I want every man to pull himself together and give his best. You younger lads, we're relying on you now. The old fellows will all be needing a bit of help. Off you go, Kit, and fetch them all here.'

It was a long time before they all assembled. Many of them were beginning to feel the effects of their long entombment. One or two of the older men could not walk very well; Jossie, who had been borne up for a while by the return to his old cavil, and by his relief at finding that after all he had not been visited by a ghost, was taken ill and had to be supported; and there was one boy who was delirious. But the rest rallied when they heard what Mr Blenkinsop had to say, and set off on their next journey with new courage.

It was an astonishing journey. At the head of the long column went Kit and Dick, with the Overman close behind them; after the leaders came a long thin column of men picking their way through the narrow gallery like a file of ants. Here and there the roof sagged ominously, and word had to be sent back for more timber to shore it up. In other places the way had cracked, leaving crevices; in others the walls seemed to have been pressed together so that there was scarce room for a man to squeeze through. The air grew fouler and fouler, and some of the men fainted. They had to be sent back to recover, and the Overman passed back a message to ask those in the rear to slow down, and not press upon the van. Dick and many who were with him began to suffer from headache and blurred vision. Mr Blenkinsop could see that at last many of the men were beginning to lose the will to win through. Then, just at that moment, when Dick and Kit had passed a dozen chalk marks, and felt that they were within striking distance of the staple, they came to the second fall. Once more the escape route was totally blocked.

Like travellers in a desert who have been kept going only by the hope of water, and who reach the oasis only to find that the wells are dry, the miners felt all hope and courage leave them at once. Dick, who now seemed to be feverish, had to lie down. Mr Blenkinsop, who had shown a wonderful example of cool and sensible leadership, suddenly collapsed; and word went round that old Jossie Milburn was in a poor way. Of all the men it was young Kit whose spirit did not fail.

'Listen,' he said, 'we're only a cockstride away now. I know it, I can tell you. I've counted my chalk marks and I'm certain that there's no more than a hundred yards atween us and the staple. Give me that pick, Alec. I'll go through the lot myself afore I'll be beat. Pass the rammel back as fast as ye can. Who'll stand by to spell me?'

'I'm here, Kit,' said Alec. 'Gan on, lad, I'm standing behind you.'

Kit made little impression, and had to give up after two minutes; but Alec took his place, and a third followed, and a fourth. Whoever could find energy timbered up the roof for them, and passed back as best they could the loose rubble that was cleared away. Four, five, six hours passed, until suddenly Kit, who was back at work, gave a shout.

'Put your hand there, Alec, will you?'

'Here?'

'Aye. Can you feel anything, or have I gone daft?'

'I can feel cold air.'

'So can I, Alec. Man, we're nearly through. Give me the pick, and by the living harry I'll get through or I'll drop.'

A few minutes later he fell exhausted, but he had broken through, and the word was sent back. There was no cheering, but never till his dying day did Alec forget that moment when a cool wind suddenly blew in through the hole, and behind him he could hear the long line of men stirring like leaves in the life-giving air.

When Kit had recovered he and Alec went through the gap. A few yards farther on they stood at the foot of the staple, and knew that they were safe.

Before he began on the last climb to safety, Kit went back to look at Dick. He was still feverish, and could hardly stand on his feet.

'Look after that lad,' he said to the men around him. 'If it hadn't been for him, there's not one of us that would have seen daylight again.'

17

The Return

On Thursday night Mr and Mrs Ullathorne, after one
more day of vain waiting, had gone to bed. By that time
most of the people of Branton had given up hope. Tem-
porary winding-gear had been rigged over the ruined shaft,
and every available man had taken a turn at clearing the
immense amount of rubble that still choked it; but the
women no longer stood around the pithead and watched
them. All they hoped now was that the bodies would be
recovered soon and brought to bank for decent burial. Not
one sound had been heard from below, not one intimation
that there was any living creature there. To all intents and
purposes the men and boys had already been buried. Mr
Sleath had not dared to visit the colliery. He had made no
public appearance at all, not even in chapel, and no one
knew where he was. No one even mentioned his name.
Grief had not yet given way to resentment.

That night a deep silence lay over the colliery. It was as
if the pit, that noisy untiring monster, had itself died. The
shops were silent. No tankies fussed up and down the
sidings. The belts, the pumps, the condenser – all were at
a standstill. The only activity was the antlike labour of the
small band of rescue men who went up and down the
broken shaft, lifting the debris piece by piece and sending
their minute loads to the surface. As they worked on, the

rest of the colliery slept and prepared once more for life.

Just before dawn, however, Mrs Ullathorne woke. The night had barely begun to give way to day. When she opened her eyes she saw that the blue-black square of the window had turned faintly grey. She did not know what had waked her, but the same impulse made her get out of bed, put on a coat and go downstairs. The stairboards were cold to her feet, but the flags in the kitchen were even colder, and she kept to the mats as far as she could. The fire in the kitchen had gone out long ago, and the cold air of the September morning entered through the crack under the door. She shivered, but something made her open the door and look out. The air outside was surprisingly still. The stars were glittering brilliantly, and dark pools had gathered behind them as they do just before morning. Beyond the garden where the fields sloped down to the railway line the early autumn mist was lying in long levels ... and through the mist, as if wading through water, there came towards her the figure whose presence had wakened her. Anyone else who had seen this figure staggering exhausted out of the morning, with blackened face and glittering white eyes, would have taken it for a spirit. But she recognized it. It was her son.

It was Kit, Kit who had always been the first in the struggle to escape, who had been the first to climb the staple and see the upper world once more, and who was the first to bring the news that the men were safe.

No one who lived through that morning ever forgot it. In the cold early dawn the women came running through the mist with food and drink and blankets; the men ran with stretchers and ropes; and the boys climbed into the trees so that they might see more clearly the men emerging one by one from the hole in the ground; and as the rescued men were reunited to those who had given them up for dead, as they were carried or supported back to the homes which they had thought they would never see again, the sun itself rose, as if it too were glad to come up out of the darkness, and shone with unclouded brilliance on the long files of rejoicing people. The blinds were drawn and the fires lit, and the smoke went up from every chimney like a sacrifice.

Dick had had to be carried up the steep steps of the staple. He had lost consciousness just before they had reached freedom; but before they could undress him and get him into bed he opened his eyes.

'Da,' he said, 'have you taken my stockings off yet?'

'We haven't taken anything off.'

'Feel inside my stocking, will you, Da?'

'Thy stocking? What on earth for?'

'There's something in there.'

'What is it, lad?'

'It's a mouse.'

'A mouse? – I think he must be a bit delirious, Hetty. Which leg?'

'I think it's the right leg. Have you got it?'

'Aye, here it is.'

'Is it still alive?'

'Just about.'

'Let it off in the garden, will you, Da?'

'If you like, lad.'

'Has it gone?'

'Aye, it's nipped off smarter than I thought it would. What made you put that in your stocking-leg?'

'I picked it up just before we got out. I thought that if we got out I'd see that it got away too.'

'You're a funny lad, Dick, that you are. But up to bed now, and you'll be as right as rain in a few days.'

Dick, however, did not recover as quickly as his father foretold. His mother nursed him carefully, but whatever it was that had struck him in the pit did not easily leave him, and Mrs Ullathorne was compelled to call in the doctor. She took this step with reluctance, for the people of Branton did not easily seek for medical help. They preferred to rely on their own cures, and on a few well-tried patent medicines. More often than not, they simply ignored their ailments, and refused to give in to them, acting on the belief that if they only kept going most weaknesses would 'backen themselves', as they said.

Dr Mackintosh, the colliery doctor, was an able man, but he never bothered to hide his contempt for the poor people among whom he worked. He was a brusque man, who pushed open the doors of his patients' houses as if he were entering a byre or a stable. When he came to see Dick, he lifted the sneck and walked without apology or greeting into the kitchen, puffing at the cigar that he always smoked when he entered a miner's house.

'Where's this lad?'

'I've got him upstairs, doctor,' replied Mrs Ullathorne. She always stood in great awe of Dr Mackintosh.

Still puffing, and without removing his hat, he stamped upstairs and looked at Dick.

'What's he been doing to get like this?'

'He took bad in the pit, doctor.'

'He took bad, did he? Let me feel your pulse, boy. Were you one of the fellows caught down there?'

'Yes, doctor.'

'Well, do you know what you've done? You've caught yourself a nice dose of rheumatic fever.'

'Will he get over it, doctor?'

'Oh he'll get over it, if he's treated sensibly.'

'I'm bonny and glad he'll be all right. I've nearly lost him once. I don't want to see him go now.'

'He won't peg out, if that's what you're worried about, but he won't be the same – you know that, don't you? He'll come out of this with a weak heart. And my advice is – keep him out of the pit. Get him some light work somewhere.'

'But where can you find that, doctor?'

'That's not my affair. I'll see that he comes round, but you'll have to see that he doesn't strain himself. If he goes down a pit again, I may as well tell you now – he'll never come out alive.'

'That's bad news for us, doctor.'

'Look after him and get him on his feet. Then send him up to me and I'll examine him again. But I'm not going to mince matters. If his heart is not affected, it will be a miracle.'

18

A New Life

Slowly the long winter passed. The damaged shaft was repaired, and, once Mr Sleath had been compelled to resign as managing-director, work on the second shaft was resumed. The new directors were in no mood for cherishing old grievances. Their chief desire was to restore the good name of the colliery; and with this in mind they bought new equipment, observed very carefully the Government's safety regulations, and tore up Mr Sleath's infamous black list. It was hinted to Mr Ullathorne that if he wished to return to the pit his old job was waiting for him. He was not slow to take the hint.

It was a great day when he prepared once more for work. He began with the night shift, and both wife and son were determined to see him off.

'Are you excited, Da?' asked Dick.

'Why, not exactly excited. I'm pleased, but I'm not off to a chapel treat, you know. Is my bait ready, Hetty? That pit bottle doesn't run out, does it?'

'I bet you'll be stiff tomorrow.'

'I bet I will. Mind, my hands should be hard enough.'

'Let's have a look at them.'

He showed Dick his hands. He had little blue rings tattooed round two fingers, and the pads of his palm were hard and calloused.

'I've kept them in shape, I think. It'll be my back that

will give me jip.'

'You'll soon get used to it.'

'Aye, it's not a bad cavil that they've given me. Has Nick gone past yet, Hetty?'

'There's plenty time. The buzzer hasn't gone yet.'

'Did you put my slush cap in my pocket?'

'Ee, by sangs, I clean forgot it.'

'Mind these pit boots have kept in grand fettle, Hetty. They're as soft as patent leather. Listen, is that Nick?'

'Is tha ready, Davy?' called a voice from outside.

'I'm just coming, Nick. Take care, Hetty.'

'Take care, Da.'

'I will.'

Outside the buzzer blew. Dick heard the familiar clump of heavy boots across the yard, and the sound of the gate closing. His father had gone.

It is a hard job for a miner to go back to work after being idle for a long time. Hard though Mr Ullathorne's hands were, they bled for the first few days, and his back and shoulders ached with every swing of the pick. After a week, however, the stiffness began to leave him, and he felt himself to be once more what he had been before that ill-fated strike – a powerful, almost tireless hewer of the old school, capable of sitting hour by hour on his little cracket, prising down great lumps of hard coal, and filling tub after tub, with no more sustenance than a few slices of bread and a bottle of cold tea.

It was a long cold winter, and a weaker boy than Dick might have gone under; but he was used to hard weather and did not shrink from it. To huddle over a fire had never been his idea of pleasure. Kit and Mr Fairless had taught him to love the pure air of the fells, and he did not forget their teaching. The fine westerly winds were medicine to him, and as he walked he felt himself growing stronger. His father, a little conscience-stricken at having taken him from school so early and having exposed him at so young an age to the dangers of the pit, gave him his freedom, and put no pressure on him to return. Besides, Mr Ullathorne was beginning to realize that there was more in the boy than he had thought, and was content to let him mark time.

This breathing space did Dick the world of good. The fresh air tanned his pale pit-boy's skin and gave him an appetite. He began to grow fast; every week his jacket seemed to grow tighter and his trousers shorter; and with the return of his bodily strength his mind grew even more alert. With the pocket money he got for doing odd jobs in the colliery he bought books. The shelves of Mr Fairless's bookcase began to fill, and the bureau was in constant use. He went back to the subjects he had liked at school, pushed on with arithmetic and began on algebra. He found that he liked making notes of all that he had seen, and of many of the things he read. He spent hours poring over an encyclopaedia that he had picked up on the second-hand stall at Durham, and even worked on his own at a tattered old Latin primer he bought for a penny.

He was changing. His mind was beginning to fill with hopes and aspirations that he could hardly himself understand. He was beginning to realize that in some important way he was not like his father and mother, or even like Kit; and at first this realization made him shy and confused. A different destiny seemed to be calling him, but he hardly knew what it was, and there seemed no one to help him to find it. Many a fine evening he would sit watching the sunlight go slowly out of the west, seeing all the colliery houses seeming to turn to do homage to the declining light. The wind brushed over the rough grass, and all round the bare landscape, plumes of grey smoke rose from the colliery chimneys; and the sound of the lapwings turning and crying in the spring air seemed to be the voice of his loneliness.

He had put off returning to the doctor's, but in the end he put aside his misgivings, and went. He knew that he had almost recovered from the effects of the accident, but he was fearful of what Dr Mackintosh might say to him.

Like most of the men he had a great dislike of the colliery surgery. As soon as he entered his distaste almost made him retreat, but his new-found courage kept him there. The surgery was cold and fusty. None of the patients was allowed to smoke, but the fumes from the doctor's cigar drifted over the partition and lay in thin blue levels around the single, naked little bulb that lit the room. From beyond the partition came the sounds of medicine bottles being filled, sinks being flushed, metal instruments dropping on to trays. The little room was unusually full. The people of Branton prided themselves on being hardy, but the severe northern winter and a crop of accidents had driven many to the doctor. They sat stiffly on the hard benches, stoical and silent, awed and uncomfortable.

Dick had to wait a long time, but his turn came round at last. He went through the partition, and waited for the doctor to turn round and attend to him.

'Now, what's up with you? Do you want a note to stop work as well? Every man-jack in the colliery seems to want a note this week. What's the matter with the lot of you?'

He thrust his face forward, and Dick noticed the long nicotine stain that dyed his moustache and travelled faintly up the right lobe of his nostrils.

'I don't want a note, doctor. I've had rheumatic fever,

and you said I had to come to be examined.'

'Were you one of the lads caught in the pit? Are you the lad that lives in the cottage next to Albert Johnson's farm?'

'Yes, sir.'

'Hmm . . . Take your coat and your shirt off. Do you never wear a vest?'

'No, sir.'

'You people are the limit! But come on, turn round.'

The doctor put the ends of his stethoscope into his ears and bent over him. When Dick was facing him, he could see the nicotine stain very clearly, like a little brown flame running up the nostril. The doctor sounded him, undid his stethoscope, and picked up his cigar.

'What's your name?'

'Dick Ullathorne, doctor.'

'Is that the name you were christened?'

'No, sir, Richard's my proper name.'

'Then why don't you give your proper name? Who was it that said you had a weak heart?'

'You did, doctor.'

'Did I? How long ago?'

'Last September.'

'Well, you seem to have got over it. Your mother been feeding you up, eh? Not much wrong with your ticker now.'

'Do you mean I can go back to work in the pit?'

'Don't see why not. Another few weeks and you should be right as a trivet. But let me give you some advice. For God's sake wear a vest, boy. It's not civilized to go around as you young folks do. What are you waiting for? Next!'

Dick walked home in a strange state of mind. He was

excited at learning that his heart was no longer weak, and he ran for a hundred yards just to reassure himself that he could run without danger. Yet somehow the news that he could go back to work in the pit brought no pleasure to him. A year ago it would have thrilled him, but now he did not entirely welcome it. He was not a coward. Not even the grim experiences of the past year had made him afraid of the pit. The truth was that he no longer wanted to work there. He did not want to let the pit close over him. Now he wanted another life.

He did not go home after leaving the doctor's surgery. Instead he went to see his grandmother, whom he found at her favourite task of cleaning the cutlery. She must have had the same knives all her married life, but now after years of rubbing with emery-paper they had worn down and were like penknives. They were very thin and the fine steel bent as she pressed on them.

'Grandma,' Dick said, taking his place at the table beside her, 'were the Ullathornes always pitmen?'

'Good Lord, no. What ever put that idea into your head?'

'I don't know. Grandda's a pitman. My father's a pitman. Kit's a pitman. We're all pitmen.'

'My father wasn't a pitman. He was a tradesman, and when I was young we lived in Kent. And your grand-dad wasn't born here. When he was younger he worked on a farm in Suffolk.'

'Is that why you have that book on horses?'

'Yes, it's your grand-dad's, not mine. But why are you asking me these questions?'

'Because I don't want to be a pitman, either.'

'You couldn't if you wanted to, could you?'

'Yes, I could; I've been to the doctor's and he says there's nothing wrong with my heart, I can start any day – but I don't want to, Grandma.'

His grandmother was the first person to whom he had made this confession, and he watched her anxiously as he spoke. He saw no change in her expression. She seemed scarce to have heard. Yet, although he did not know it, he had spoken the words that she had waited for fifty years to hear. Inwardly she exulted, and resolved that he would not go without her help.

But what Dick stood urgently in need of was something that she could hardly give. It was guidance. He had come to the end of one road, but did not know where the other began; and she was too old and too friendless to direct him.

Dick's father and mother were equally helpless.

They were not surprised when he told them that he did not want to return to the pit, and they were far too fond of him and too proud of him to oppose him; but they were puzzled.

'We'll not stand in your light, bonny lad,' said his father. 'Kit and me can bring enough in for your mother to manage on. But what do you fancy instead of the pit?'

'I don't know.'

'It'll be a bit of a job to find anything. Easy jobs dinna fall off the trees.'

'It isn't an easy job I want. I'm not frightened of work. But I'm not made for the pit, Da.'

'There's not much else but pit-work here. But we'll keep our eyes open. We'll find an opening somewhere.'

When Dick gave vague answers like these to his father and mother he felt vexed and confused; but slowly his bewilderment began to give way to resolution. By now he knew that he had a quick brain. He knew that learning came easily to him. He could remember clearly, and think clearly, and already in his imagination he was beginning to explore far beyond the bounds of the colliery. Now he was beginning to reap the benefits of the good tuition of Mr Bradwell, and the companionship of Peter and Mr Fairless. He was resolved to break free. Then one day he came upon a book in which there was an account of the opening of the burial chamber on Branton Hill. It was by Mr Candlin, and as soon as he saw the name he remembered Mr Candlin's last words to him. He remembered too how once he had tried to see Mr Sleath, and how his fear had made him miss his chance of speaking to him. He suddenly made up his mind to go to Mr Candlin and ask for his help. He knew where he lived. Once when they had been walking along the Bailey on their way to the cathedral Mr Fairless had pointed it out to him.

He took the way that he had taken a long time before when he had gone shopping with his mother and father. He left the main road at Grey Bridge, and climbed to the top of Observatory Hill. To his right, lost somewhere among the trees, was Sion House. Dick had heard that Mr Sleath had sold it and had left the district, and as he looked he wondered what had happened to the strong, deaf old man who had been a servant there. But he had no desire to see Sion House again. He turned away and looked at the little gatehouse he had used to admire, and the trees behind it, and the cathedral on its promontory. This magnificent scene always excited him, and he began to jog happily down the steep slopes of Observatory Hill. Then he crossed the bridge and found himself at the entry to the Bailey.

The street had always held a great fascination for him. The entry was spanned by a high arch, and from its crumbling masonry trailed fronds and creepers. As Dick passed under the arch his rough boots began to ring on the cobbles and the sound seemed to echo from the blank façades of the houses. He felt ashamed of making such a noise, and if a venerable porter had crept out of an archway and told him it was he that was rousing the jackdaws that chacked around the cathedral tower, he would have believed him and apologized.

But no one disturbed him and he passed along the quiet street until he came to Mr Candlin's house. It was a plain house, but well proportioned, possessing a fine doorway, and a beautiful shining knocker shaped like a dolphin. Once he had passed the house at night and glimpsed a big kitchen with bright copper utensils ranged on a tall dresser. This bright kitchen, the gleaming copper kettles, the lovely polished knocker had seemed to him the symbols of a life of ease and beauty that he had never known; and when he lifted his hand to the dolphin he had once more the feeling of being an intruder. There came over him once more the cowardice that had paralysed him as he had looked at Sion House, but now he knew that he had to go on. He lifted his hand and knocked.

Mr Candlin was in, and as soon as Dick entered the room he knew he had been recognized.

'It's Richard Ullathorne – my little archaeologist from Branton. Come in, Richard, come in,' he said, and held out his hand as he always did, with the thumb sticking out stiffly from the wide-open palm.

'Not so little now, eh?' he went on. 'And not so pale either. Something tells me that you didn't let the pit close

184

over you after all.'

'I nearly did, Mr Candlin.'

'Were you among those buried there?'

'Yes.'

'Amazing. Here I am – nearly fifty. You'll be lucky if you're fifteen. Yet you must have gone through more in those three days in that mine than I've gone through in a lifetime. But what are you doing for yourself now?'

'Nothing.'

'Nothing?'

'I mean, I don't work in the pit any more. I caught rheumatic fever, and the doctor said I hadn't to work underground any more. I'm better now, but I still don't work at the pit.'

'Do you mean you can't get work – or you don't want to?'

Dick paused.

'I don't think I want to, Mr Candlin.'

'Ah,' said Mr Candlin, drawing out the syllable. 'I wondered how long it would be before this happened. Sit back in your chair, Dick, and tell me all about yourself.'

'I've changed, Mr Candlin. Once I wanted to be like my father and my brother, but somehow I've changed. I don't quite know how to say it, but going down the pit would be like going to prison now.'

'I understand you, my boy. You want to escape. You want to do what I did forty years ago. My father, Dick, was a bricklayer, and he wanted me to be a bricklayer too ... but I wouldn't, and I didn't. But it's not easy to escape. The pit will take you, and it will expect nothing but strong muscles and a good heart. But to climb you must learn.'

'I haven't been idle, Mr Candlin. I always remembered what you told Peter and me about learning. I've worked.'

'What have you been doing?'

'Arithmetic, and a bit of algebra. Writing. Even a little bit of Latin.'

'Latin?'

'Yes, sir.'

'All by yourself?'

'Yes, sir.'

'How far have you got?'

'I can't say.'

'Let's find out. Here, try this little sentence out of Caesar. Can you translate that?'

'I think so.'

'Do it then.'

It was a simple sentence and Dick translated it quickly.

'Well done, Richard. By jingo, you have pluck! But I always knew it. Has anybody ever told you what remarkable eyes you have?'

'Yes, sir. My grandmother's brother once said something about them.'

'Then he must have been a very astute man. I haven't much influence, Richard. Scholars like us never meet many important people. But give me your address, and if anything can be done, I'll do it. That Latin of yours, it may do the trick. You must spend the evening with me, and we'll talk about our absent friends, eh? And you must tell me all that you've been doing since we said good-bye to them.'

They drew up their chairs to the fire and talked. The gas hissed softly against the mantles, and its pale, friendly light fell on the tall bookcases, the square vases ranged on

186

the shelves, the gilt clock on the mantelpiece, the brass handles on Mr Candlin's desk. Dick sat awkwardly in the big wing-chair that Mr Candlin had given him; he was more used to the hard forms and crackets of a colliery kitchen. But the kindly scholar gently put him at his ease. He talked about his own life, about his work, and his friendship with Mr Fairless; and as Dick walked home that night along the Bailey he was no longer abashed by the echoes from his clumsy boots. He set his heels smartly on the cobbles, and strode confidently and rapidly up the steep slope out of the city.

Mr Candlin kept his word. A few days later Dick received a letter asking him to go and see a Mr Dorman who kept a chemist's shop in Saddler Street. Once more he set out on a journey that was now familiar to him.

The interview took place in the shop, with the old chemist sitting on a stool on one side of the counter and Dick standing on the other.

'What did you say your age was, Richard?' asked Mr Dorman. He had a heavy face with a bald head more like a cone than a dome, and heavy cheeks that sagged.

'Fourteen gone, sir.'

'You're a bit young.'

'Yes, but I'm eager to learn, Mr Dorman.'

'Yes, but eagerness isn't knowledge, my boy. Now then, I want you to answer these questions. Can you drive a pony and trap?'

'Yes, sir, I've worked with horses.'

'Can you find your way about the countryside? How many miles is it, for instance, from here to Towin Law?'

'I should say about twelve by the main road, sir.'

'Tell me the way you'd take.'

'Grey Bridge, Branton, past Standalone, past Moseley Terrace, and then Towin Law.'

'Have you missed anything out?'

'I think I forgot Sunnyhaugh.'

'Do you know anything about drugs and medicines?'

'Not much, sir.'

'Hmm, that's a handicap, you know. But Mr Candlin tells me you know a bit of Latin. Well, that will be useful. Now look up at those boxes, and then turn away.'

Dick looked up and saw a row of little drawers let into the wall above the counter. He took in the names quickly – Senna, Friar's Balsam, Witch Hazel, Camomile, Spirits of Ammonia.

'Now repeat them.'

He repeated them with little difficulty. It was not easy for him to forget fine-sounding names like those.

'Yes, you have a good memory, and I've been told you can write a fair letter. Well now, Richard Ullathorne, I'll tell you what I want doing. I have a good little business, and it's growing. There are places all over this county that want drugs and medicines, and I can provide them. I want a good journeyman, a lad that can drive a pony and trap, deliver my goods, learn the business, keep accounts ... ah yes, that's reminded me of something. Do this little sum, will you? Take your time. I'm not interested in speed, but in accuracy. Finished already? Hmm. It's correct, too. That's very good. Now just let me listen to that heart of yours, will you?'

Dick undid his coat and shirt, and Mr Dorman put an old-fashioned stethoscope on him, and listened. As Dick was being examined, he took in the unusual scene – the pale yellow gaslight burning over the counter and shining on the brass scales, the shapely bottles of coloured water, the pills and powders. He breathed the flavours of the herbs that lay boxed around him, and felt himself at last on the threshold of his new world.

'Hmm ... Nothing wrong there, anyhow,' said Mr Dorman, unhooking his stethoscope. 'Well, young man, I'm prepared to take you on. But it's not just an assistant I want. I want a journeyman apprentice, and something more even than that. I'm looking for somebody who's prepared to do a lot of training, and the more he does, the more he'll get out of it in the end ... But, wait a bit, boy, there's one more party to be consulted before the deal is done. Come with me.'

Dick followed with some misgiving. He had not expected to have to meet another partner, and felt a little dashed.

Mr Dorman took a lamp, lit it, led him out of the shop by the back way and across a yard. Then, flinging open a door he shone his lamp upon a black pony lying patiently in the straw.

'There's my partner, Dick, and now she's yours. What do you think of her?'

Dick hardly knew what to say. The little pony was the image of Bonny, the Bonny he had loved and left to die in the pit. He was glad that the stable was dark.

There was one thing about this appointment that neither Dick nor Mr Candlin ever knew. Before Dick met Mr Dorman, someone else had had an interview with him. It was old Mrs Ullathorne; but what passed between her and the chemist, she never told. It was one more of her secrets, and no one ever knew how she had smoothed the way for her beloved grandson to escape from the pit.

19

Conclusion

A fortnight later, Dick went out on his first journey. During that fortnight Mr Dorman had tested him, and found him to be all that Mr Candlin had claimed him to be. Now he was giving him his first commission. Dick was to deliver a consignment of medicines to the remote, high village of Towin Law, twelve miles away.

He had slept at his employer's, and at first light he harnessed the pony, loaded the trap, and set off over the cobbles of the silent city. Just over an hour later he rested his pony on the crest of the long sandy lane above Branton. It was still early morning and the rabbits were out among the heather. A gentle west wind came riding in over the undulating fells, brushing through the low twisted thorns, and turning the lapwings over like leaves. Below the lane stretched the heathery slope of the fell, falling away to the reedy field where, little more than a year ago, the strikers had pitched their tents. Beyond the field lay the allotments, and then the serried rows of the colliery streets, their damp slate roofs shining in the morning light. Dick watched the smoke rising from the hundreds of chimneys and slanting away as the wind caught it, the taller plumes ascending from the colliery chimneys, the steam rising from the great condenser, the pulley wheels turning this way and that as the cages went up and down; and as he looked he

saw in his mind's eye the men preparing for one more day of work, picking up their pit bottles and their bait-pokes, and the women making ready for one more day of cooking and cleaning and washing. Then there came to him a vision of the other population, the invisible workers already below ground, sitting naked to the waist, pulling down the walls of black coal, filling it into narrow tubs, and pushing them to the bottom of the greedy shaft – men like his father, and Kit, the strong, the patient, the poorly-paid, the happy, of whom he had himself been one.

But he could not stay long. Away to the west and across the fells rose the streets and chimneys of Towin Law. This was his new destination. As the larks sang overhead, and the heather shook in the freshening wind, he climbed back into his trap, shook up his pony, and went on.